PUNISHMENT
WITH KISSES

Visit us at www.boldstrokesbooks.com

What Reviewers Say About the Author

"To use words straight from this book, Anderson-Minshall's writing is 'fast and brash and all consuming,' describing both the kind of sex popular culture tells us women don't like to have and the kind of literature of which we need more."—Dahlia Schweitzer, author of *I've Been a Naughty Girl* and *Seduce Me*

"*Punishment with Kisses* is a smart, sticky read through a mysterious sister's secret sex diaries."—Helen Boyd, author of *She's Not the Man I Married*

"Diane Anderson-Minshall's new novel *Punishment with Kisses* explores the sexy quarter-life crises of some of fiction's most realistic dykes. These women are on a wild ride through S/M dungeons, bars, and most of all intensifying family secrets—both devastating and titillating—that left me hanging on every word."—Sassafras Lowrey, author of *GSA to Marriage: Stories of a Life Lived Queerly*

"*Punishment with Kisses* unfurls an intricate web of sexual relations laced with intrigue as young Megan parses clues in her sister's murder. Is Megan motivated to solve the crime out of a sense of justice, or is her detective work a ploy for sexual exploration and self-discovery? Anderson-Minshall handles this tension with careful consideration while providing the reader a delicious murder mystery."—Marcie Bianco, Rutgers University

By the Author

Punishment with Kisses

With Jacob Anderson-Minshall

Blind Curve

Blind Leap

Blind Faith

PUNISHMENT WITH KISSES

by

Diane Anderson-Minshall

2009

ISBN 10: 1-60282-081-3
ISBN 13: 978-1-60282-081-4

This Trade Paperback Original Is Published By
Bold Strokes Books, Inc.
P.O. Box 249
Valley Falls, NY 12185

First Edition: June 2009

Credits
Editor: Cindy Cresap
Production Design: Stacia Seaman
Cover Design By Sheri (graphicartist2020@hotmail.com)

Acknowledgments

I'd be remiss if I didn't mention William Bayer, author of the great psychosexual thriller *Punish Me With Kisses*. I read that book in eighth grade, out loud, to my new classmates at Payette Junior High, in Payette, Idaho. The kids loved my little dime store novel, so much so that Mr. Nelson, our generally laid-back English teacher, had me and the book removed from class. It was my first trip to the principal, but it was so worth it. The book got terrible reviews, though Bayer went on to write others, including the Lambda Award–winning gay mystery *The Magician's Tale* (under pen name David Hunt). Ever since I read *Punish* in the early '80s, I dreamed of a lesbian revisioning—and thankfully I got the chance here, with *Punishment with Kisses*. There is very little in common with the original but inspiration, born from my hormone-fueled adolescent fantasies and Bayer's warped words.

I get so much help with my books that I need to get better at starting a giant list at the outset, so I can note everyone along the way. Instead, here I am at the end, exhausted and mindless, trying to remember the dozens of folks who provided fabulous assistance. Thanks first, to my editors, Jennifer Knight and Cindy Cresap, and my publisher Len Barot, for sticking with me and guiding me through this publishing process yet again. All of the Bold Strokes team deserves nods from the support folks (Lori Anderson, Connie Ward) to the consultants (Paula Tighe—thanks for the Everglades) to the creatives (Sheri, Stacia Seaman) to the authors and their spouses (JLee Meyer and Cheryl Craig—thanks for many great meals!). I've forgotten more than I've remembered, so just know I owe you many thanks!

Much love and thanks to my *Curve* colleagues, who put up with my endless absences when I'm on tour, and my shameless self-promotion almost all the other times, especially my boss and friend Frances Stevens and my faithful editorial team: Katie

Peoples, Rachel Beebe, Rachel Shatto, and Flo Enriquez, Ondine Kilker, Stefanie Liang, and Diana Berry.

Thanks to Kina Williams and Sossity Chiricuzio for orchestrating my awesome author pictures yet again, and to Stacy Bias, Dustina Haas, and Lipstick and Dipstick for your creative friendships. Jeff, Corey, Tina, Athena, Erica, and anyone else I've forgotten get so much thanks—even when we go months between calls, your friendship sustains me.

Lastly, my family deserves mucho recognition (though I sincerely hope none of you are reading this book—I may wither with embarrassment). Thanks to Keith Jr. for challenging me to remember what's important; to Tanya, Jaime, and Wendy for giving me four adorable nieces and nephew; to Keith Sr., Marlene, Luanne, and Paula, for raising me; to Wayne, Judy, Michele, and Jennye for welcoming me into your family. Thanks to you all, especially Jacob.

Oh, and thanks to *Playboy* magazine circa 1979, for helping instill a sexual curiosity in my tween soul that clearly landed me a book deal twenty years later.

Dedication

To my co-pilot, the only person who knows the real me,
and married me anyway. Thank you, babe, from the bottom
of my heart.

CHAPTER ONE

I thought that summer was all about my sister's murder, but looking back I realize it was all about me. It has always been all about me. I just didn't realize it back then. When I was driving home from Tulane, I had no idea of the journey I was about to embark on. And while that voyage would take place internally, it was still far more arduous than my meandering return from college, when I was crisscrossing state lines and binge eating at truck stops and fantasizing about being ravished by lady truckers, all as a sort of psycho-celebration of my four years of fruition that came with my English degree. Back then, I was a brand spankin' new graduate with a cascading sense of self that seemed to dissolve and reappear at inappropriate times, like when I was naked or hitting on high school boys just to toy with them. I knew nothing.

Standing on Father's property five years later, knee deep in a colorful pile of leaves, the final vestiges of fall clinging to bare branches of the trees overhead, my days of college partying are distant memories. And the concerns I had then I now realize were utterly trivial. How selfish and immature I was that summer. As the final days of my sister's life trickled away, I allowed my own insecurities and petty sibling rivalry to keep me from sharing those days with her.

If I had only taken the time then to get to know her, I might have prevented her murder. I certainly would never have needed to descend into the darkness myself, spelunking like a cave explorer into my sister's secret life, and nearly getting trapped in the dank and shadowy fissures I stumbled into in search of her murderer. The truth is, I lost my way in that labyrinth and I might have lost my very soul if I hadn't discovered the one thing I least expected—true love.

Now, as I peered inside the pool house, my eyes prickled with the sting of tears. Though it's been unused since the night Ash was killed—and any trace of her has long since been removed— it still looks exactly as it did before she died. The fluid lines of the antique Queen Anne table were an ironic juxtaposition next to the Ikea Tylösand couch—the combo my sister used to jokingly call my stepmother Tabitha's Swedish-Amish-Americana design style.

In those days, I was so caught up in my own jealous anxiety I failed to notice that even while she was still alive Ash never seemed to be a part of her surroundings. It was as if she were floating atop them, moving through everything—furniture, people, life—as if she were a mere ghostly apparition. And yet, while she was living on the surface, never embracing us, it was as though life couldn't help but absorb her. Everyone she met seemed to be changed somehow by the experience, by her very presence.

Though it's drained for the oncoming winter and littered with piles of withered crimson and gold leaves, the pool still reminds me of Ash, too. One squint of my eyes and I can still imagine her next to it, sprawled on a lounge chair, slathered in Hawaiian Tropic tanning oil, the scent of evaporating coconut wafting through the air, admirers and margaritas by her side. She was all coy smiles and forced laughter, swimming in a sea of sex, sun, and pulchritude. No one, least of all me, seemed to notice she was drowning.

I was tempted to dip my hand in the pool, to scoop up a handful of damp leaves, no doubt coated on the underside with a fine mist of sludge, and play a modern version of "loves me not." Except I'd replace *love* with *forgive*. In the last five years, I've thought of nothing more than whether my sister would forgive me for failing her in her final days. I was so green, like the delicate buds that emerge from the tree limbs in the warm days of spring. I was so fresh from college and so riddled with my own baggage that I could never see Ash for who she was, only who I imagined her to be. Even now, I don't know that I understand entirely what happened, or why. How culpable was I in her death? I don't know that I will ever know for certain. I don't know if I want to.

What I do know is that I've spent the last half decade mourning a sister I was too selfish to really know and feeling nothing but regret about how I treated her. This shame and guilt was a logjam in my life, stalling my personal relationships and my career. I had pissed off employers and lovers with equal casualness, and until I hit my stride in therapy it looked like I was going to die an angry, two-timing coffee jockey instead of becoming the person I am.

Closure. It's a mythical word. And almost impossible to find.

"Megan!" Our housekeeper Maria woke me from my reverie. She must have spied me through the greenhouse doors. "I didn't know you'd be home today. Are you here for the weekend? Come inside. Do you need help with your bags?" Maria gushed with questions, lobbing each out rapid fire like a dart on a barroom wall before I even had a chance to open my mouth. She didn't know the full story. How could she? I was barely able to understand it myself. I do know, like many tragedies, it all started with sex— which meant different things to Ash and me.

That summer I came home, I wasn't a virgin, but I certainly wasn't the woman around town my sister Ash was. I'd spent most of college with my nose in a book, save for those few nights with

Terra Moscowitz, which began innocently enough with us in her dorm room dry humping each other after a Take Back the Night rally that devolved into so much more. I'm not sure what it was about anti-rape rallies, but they certainly seemed to make Terra horny. Sadly, her girlfriend was around half the time, which meant I got leftover, hand-me-down sex—but I was happy to have it.

Sex with Terra was fast and brash and all consuming, the kind that popular culture tells us women don't like to have. She could wield a strap-on like it was an extension of her body, and I guess in Terra's case, with the frequency with which she wielded it, it probably was.

Terra was one of only three lovers I had while away at college. Terra, Andrea, and Mark. Andrea wore heavy kohl eyeliner and black turtlenecks year round. She regularly drank bathtub gin, forgot her bipolar meds daily, and frequently told me, *in flagrante,* that when it came to lovemaking, I would never please another woman. Since I could never please *her* during our brief, clumsy encounters, I began to suspect she was right. Why *were* women so hard to please?

That question, of course, led me to Mark, the hairy pre-med student who wasn't hard to please at all. After a few minutes of kissing, when he'd shove his tongue down my throat until I choked, I'd pop off my bra—because his thick fingers seemed too clumsy to handle the small clasps—and well, Mark would pop off too. I think he made it inside me only once during our frequent attempts. The rest of the time he left the field before I even got to the game. It was nice being wanted—and more than that, being so exciting to a partner that he couldn't even wait for the main act—after Terra's unavailability and Andrea's unkind endorsements—but even when Mark was there for me, there was no thrill in the moment.

His facial hair hurt everything it touched, particularly my nether regions where it seemed to attach to—and rip away from—my personal undergrowth as though it were Velcro. His knowledge of female anatomy was alarming, especially for someone planning to become a doctor. The last time he went down on me, giving my nappy dugout sloppy circular kisses that missed the mark every single repetition—*God, why couldn't he find my clitoris?*—he gave up, breathless and exhausted before I'd begun to feel even a twinge of desire. I gyrated my hips left and right and yanked him into position by his hair, but *nothing* seemed to work.

Which led me back to Terra's embrace and her sloppy strap-on seconds. It was enough to drive me to the brink of ecstasy each time, even though she shoved me out of bed the minute we finished so I'd escape before her girlfriend returned. I think it was a thrill for Terra, the fear of getting caught, but it would've been nice, just once, to lie there for a moment after we finished, basking in the rush of blood to my head, the sweat pooling between us, gazing at her flushed face and sticky smile.

Alas, with graduation upon us, Terra went east and I went west, and the next time I heard from her was alongside a wedding announcement, heralding the Massachusetts nuptials of her and the girlfriend. Why is it that the biggest cheaters are the quickest to jump on the wedding bandwagon? Is there excitement in the challenge of commitment? Is it even more thrilling to cheat after you've said *I do*?

My journey to love took a lot longer than Terra's. My long, circuitous drive home to Lake Oswego offered a psychic buffer, the spiritual cleansing I needed before submitting to an entire summer in close proximity with a family I considered toxic. Against all evidence to the contrary, I still hoped that maybe *this* would be the summer my sister Ash and I rekindled the relationship we'd had years ago, when we were both pre-teens. Back when our mother was still alive. Back before Father took a child bride and Ash was a college dropout, before all our paths diverged in such nuanced ways.

Little did I know then the twists and turns my personal, psychological journey would take—around dangerous curves, over treacherous roads, down dark alleys and dead-end streets—

or that by the time I reached my destination, my relationship with myself, my sexuality, and my family would be forever altered.

❖

"I don't fucking care what you think!" Ash yelled, her top completely naked, the bottom of her bikini riding up around her ass. She flaunted her body just to hurt me, to remind me that compared to her ample bosoms and perfectly proportioned bottom, I had the body of an ogre.

Ashley always was the beautiful one, a woman every man wanted. Every woman wanted her too, I was sure, though they were probably more cautious about admitting it. Ash—as I'd called her since we were kids—seemed to sense early on what power her allure would hold over others. As soon as she hit puberty, Ash was wielding her sexuality like a modern-day Lolita. I envied her confidence. I was always zit faced and fatter than the other kids, developing love handles before I got boobs, and even then there was a pudgy roundness about me that still looked unformed well into my college years. But Ash sprang from sixth grade a full-fledged woman, a sexual Pied Piper with a legion of fans who would gladly do her bidding merely for a chance to be near her.

Ash seemed to have no shame when it came to displaying her body. She had no qualms about being nearly nude, save for a tiny black bikini thong, even when standing in the kitchen, with the cook and our maid Maria and the gardener whose name I didn't know then. Worse, Ash seemed equally comfortable exposed in front of me and our father and his wife Tabitha—who I then thought of as the stepmonster—who was no longer a child bride but, at twenty-eight, was still just two years older than Ash. Father was absolutely enraged by each and every spectacle involving his exhibitionist nymph of a daughter.

Indeed, at this moment, our father, Bradford Caulfield, a man usually so rigid and silent we hardly noticed his appearance, had beads of perspiration rolling down the sides of his contorted face, one thin blue vein bulging below his collar, hidden mostly by the formal shirtsleeves he was wearing. His fists were balled up at his sides.

"If you continue down this path of moral bankruptcy, Ashley Spencer Caulfield, you *will* regret it."

The threat could be taken as nothing but that. Except pigheaded Ash couldn't have cared less. As Father raged on, threatening her rather malevolently, Ash started fighting back, almost berating him like an ex-lover, while Tabitha, usually so flighty and flirty, stared on doe-eyed and aghast.

It was just another day in Casa de Caulfield. But maybe this time Ash had crossed the line.

"Listen, Daddy-O, my sexuality is my own damn business. It's not yours to control." Ash said each word in a constrained manner. Too much weed, probably, slowing down her reflexes.

"This is my house and I won't have you swimming naked in front of the help and whoring around with an endless parade of misfits and freaks. For fuck's sake, Ashley, what are you thinking? This will be all over town and then you'll never get in the Junior League."

Ash doubled over laughing. It was maniacal the way she responded to Father's reprimand. The coercion that would make me back down always emboldened Ash. Today was no different.

"Oh yes, must not upset the frigid bitches of the society pages—" Ash began. She clearly didn't care about the Junior League, and I was surprised that Father hadn't already surmised it.

He cut her off. "That's it. You're out of the house. If you're going to behave like a pig, you can move into the pool house. Let's see how you like living in eight hundred square feet with no one to serve you." Father made the pronouncement as though sentencing Ash to the confines of a small shed, not a vacation cabana with its own Olympic-size swimming pool. That's the way things worked when you were the golden child. If these were criminal proceedings, Ashley Caulfield would have just been sent to a ritzy, resort-like white-collar minimum security prison. If the shoe was on the other foot, and it was me in that position, I'm certain the ruling would be completely different. I'd be sent straight to Sing Sing.

Ash stared at him for a minute, as though pausing to catch up with what he was saying, or simply planning out her summer of fun. Then she turned and left, casting one last snide comment over her shoulder. "Oh, Father, don't be silly. *I* won't have any problem finding someone to service me."

The next day half a dozen people arrived and began moving Ash's belongings into the pool house. I was still pissed off at Ash for ruining my homecoming and for putting a kibosh on any chance of the two of us bonding before I headed to grad school or out into the real world—I wasn't exactly sure yet which course I was going to take. Ash's acts of selfish defiance also effectively eliminated any chance I could have the summer I'd dreamt of, lounging by the pool myself.

With her banishment to the cabana Father established a no-fly zone, a walled East Berlin in the center of our property. To cross the border between our house and the pool would now be seen by Father as an act of treason, an announcement of my alliance with his sworn enemy. The retaliation would be swift and severe. And with the pool house already occupied by his favorite child, God knows what would happen to me. I imagined being kicked to the curb, sent away in a cab, never allowed to return.

It was too dangerous to risk, even for a summer of deep tanning and refreshing dips in the cool blue-green water. But I was still pissed. This was my last summer at home and now I was stuck spending it all indoors, trapped inside with a pissed-off father and Tabitha, the stepmonster, who I'd never managed to get close to, even though we're not that far apart in age.

Within hours of Ash's dramatic departure from the main house, there was a wild party raging by the pool. From the balcony of my second-floor room, I could not help but see all the beautiful people wandering in and out of the pool house, some drinking, others just sunning themselves. I didn't need to find Ash in the crowd to know there would be people bunched around her, toadying all over her.

I stepped back into my room and shut the sliding doors. Ash could have her little tantrums. I was going to ignore her and her escalating war with Father by thrusting myself into all the novels I'd brought home with me. Dorothy Allison, Jewel Gomez, and Michelle Tea. These authors were like good friends I could call on for all-night gab sessions. Their words gave me the kind of excitement I wasn't finding at home and reminded me why I loved to be immersed in fiction instead of real life. A good novel is like a current that sweeps you up and carries you away from the real world to a magical land where you get to let yourself go and delve into the lives of people far more interesting than you.

With Michelle Tea's *Valencia* in hand, I stretched out across my four-poster bed, nestled in the down comforter that should be too hot for this time of year, but somehow felt cool beneath me, and let the story pull me into a fantasy world. For the first two days home I was so engrossed that I barely moved—occasionally rolling from my back to my stomach to prevent bedsores, and rising only for bathroom breaks or to go downstairs for the requisite meals.

Loud voices and laughter wafting up from the pool house interrupted my reverie. I tried to ignore the noise, but I couldn't shake my curiosity. Who was out there and what were they doing? It wouldn't hurt to stretch my legs.

Not wanting to damage the book's spine, I carefully slid a piece of paper in to hold my place and set it on my bedside table. My legs were spongy with sleep, and when I put my weight down they caved under me. I grabbed on to one of the smooth, hand-carved posts and managed to stay upright. I used the furniture as crutches while I stumbled across the room, going from bed to desk and outside to the railing of the balcony.

Fortunately, my land legs returned, because the minute I stepped outside I was blinded by the light and instinctively raised a hand to shield my pupils from the excruciating brilliance of the midday sun. When my eyes finally adjusted to the brightness, I was not surprised to see Ash wearing nothing but bikini bottoms, floating on a giant inflatable bed in the middle of our pool. She wasn't alone. A man wearing shorts and a T-shirt, and a woman with an old-fashioned one-piece suit were taking turns stroking Ash in the guise of applying sunscreen. Their movements rocked the raft and splashed water onto Ash, who shrieked theatrically. I looked around to see who was playing audience to her show. Our gardener, whose name I still couldn't pronounce, was skulking behind the hedges, pretending to trim them while peering over at Ash and her strange friends floating in the aquamarine water. She was probably trying to give the old guy a heart attack.

I was appalled at her complete lack of decorum, and angry with myself for falling for Ash's exhibitionism. She was probably out there laughing louder and louder, calculating what decibel would bring Father or me to a window. Ash was like a child having a tantrum, stamping her foot and yelling, "Look at me, look at me," to get attention.

To hell with her. *Valencia* was waiting, full of the kind of clever prose I loved to read in literature classes but had never yet managed to write myself. Tea's words saturated my mind like rain falling through slats on a barn roof. Sometimes I read lines aloud, letting the words linger on my tongue, rolling them around my mouth, tasting them with the different sensors—sweet, sour, salty. I adored her words, and I turned them over and over in my head as the day began to slip into evening, oblivious to the party still going on.

A scream interrupted me. I spit out Tea's words and tossed her book aside before racing out to the balcony again. Ash was out of the water but standing by the pool, now with a different duo: the woman from earlier today and a new man. I wanted to stare, to see what the hell they were up to that elicited the shriek I'd just heard. But I was afraid Ash would catch me at it, and I didn't want to give her the satisfaction of knowing she'd gotten my attention *again*. And knowing her, Ash would just call me a pervert and tell Father I was spying on her, just to get me in trouble.

She was always doing things like that when we were younger. I remember one time when we were kids and Ash was in trouble for something—I don't remember what, since usually it seemed like she could do no wrong. But I do remember Ash had been sent to her room alone. Even back then Ash couldn't stand to be alone. She cracked open her door and stood there whispering my name until I came to see what the fuss was.

Then Ash looked me right in the eyes and slammed her hand in the door. On purpose. She broke two of her fingers and had to go to the hospital. But her plaintive wails brought Father running and her lies convinced him I'd been responsible. Ash was released from solitary and I took her place in the doghouse, so it was a win-win situation all around for her.

I didn't want to give her that kind of satisfaction now, so instead I grabbed the pair of odd binocular-like sunglasses that were an expensive good-bye gift from Mark, who somehow thought bird watching might bring me solace in his post-graduation absence. I'd never watched a bird in my life, and I didn't intend to start, but I had realized that the spectacles appeared to others as simply a pair of peculiar looking sunglasses. No one would notice me people watching from my room, though with these telescoping super-strength lenses I could practically see every pore, every hair on each person's body.

I could stoically relax on my balcony, sit in my reclining redwood patio lounge holding my novel, and peer over the pages at Ash and what I was beginning to suspect was a constant parade of lovers. I felt simultaneously intrigued and repelled by the sight of so many of them fawning over my sister like she was an adorable but doomed SPCA puppy begging for a home. What did Ash offer that turned normally independent people into simpering fools? If I paid close attention, would I catch a glimpse of her secret ingredient? Was it something intrinsic to her soul or could I apply it like a glossy lipstick? Could it magically transform me externally, the way Tea's words did in my mind?

Ash had always enchanted other people. When we were young girls being trotted out at Father's cocktail parties for show and tell, the partygoers would always gather around sweet, pig-tailed Ash. At one of Father's office holiday parties, when Ash was maybe eight or nine, she got on stage while the band was on a break and announced that she had a special treat for the audience. She was dressed in a little red velvet pantsuit with white fur trim that my mother must have helped her pick out. I was still too terrified to speak to people unless forced, and so I stood there, slack jawed, as enamored of my sister as the rest of the audience. She was everything I wanted to be, back then and still now. Beautiful, smart, charming, and truly unafraid of anything. At the party, I kept hiding below the buffet table, stuffing my face and wondering how soon I could get out of there while Ash was charming the pants off of Father's colleagues.

Soon all eyes were on Ash as a band member handed her a microphone and she started belting out a perfect rendition of "Santa Baby." We'd been singing Christmas carols in front of the mirror in our underwear for weeks, karaoke style, so we both knew every single word. But watching Ash up there, I realized that she brought something to the song I never could. We weren't even teenagers yet, but there was something faintly womanly about Ash, like a twenty-year-old trapped in a nine-year-old's body. All eyes were on her as she winked and smiled and sang in a Betty Boop tone. When she finished, the crowd applauded and gushed and Father beamed with pride.

For years afterward, I would think of that party, of how Ash could walk into any situation and charm people. She would sometimes take me under her wing, telling me how to make an entrance like she did, but just as often she'd mock me or push me aside when others were around. Always, we seemed to be competing for Father's affection, and always, Ash won.

Even in our family, I seemed to be on the outside of Ash's world, looking on as everyone fluttered around her, flitting about and marveling.

So that summer I pretended to be a birdwatcher looking for that endangered species. I pretended I was an anthropologist observing a foreign culture, longing to learn the sacred rituals of a society I could never truly enter.

CHAPTER TWO

Hours of spying slipped into days, and I soon decided I was getting far more from observing Ash than I would ever garner from my novels and their make-believe worlds. I started bringing a notepad out to the balcony with me, jotting down random things I noticed, hoping somehow a pattern would emerge and I could unravel the secrets of this alien world. If nothing else, I told myself, this would enliven my own writing, help me infuse an element of realness that my English professors had always complained was lacking from my characters, which they criticized as being more caricatures than living, breathing, believable individuals.

Watching Ash was like viewing my own private reality dating program. Each new day brought another surprising revelation. Father, an archconservative Republican, must have been having a fit, knowing what she was doing out there, and yet he never said anything to that effect, he never went out and shut her party down. Maybe he was able to pretend it wasn't happening. Maybe going down there would have confronted him with the vulgar truth, that his little girl wasn't a little girl any longer, that she was very much an adult, a sexually aggressive woman who was hanging around the pool with all manner of riffraff, drinking and smoking pot, lighting up casually, and passing spliffs as if they were simply sharing cigarettes.

There were colorful drinks strewn about, drinks that could pass for punch, but I could tell from the way the girls giggled and tittered that there was booze in them for certain. Each new day, Ash seemed to ratchet up the poolside debauchery, as though challenging Father to step in, pushing his limits to see when he would break. Even I was surprised by his restraint. He seemed to be combating her by fighting a cold war, trying to freeze her out by utterly ignoring Ash's increasing decadence. It couldn't continue indefinitely. Eventually Ash would push him too far and Father would explode, raging as white hot as any atomic bomb. I couldn't help but wonder how many people would end up getting hurt, casualties in their little war. Would it be worth it in the end? What did she hope to prove?

I couldn't see *everything* that was happening down there by the pool, but over the next few weeks I saw enough. Cocktails drunk, joints smoked, drugs passed, and pills popped, right there, directly under Father's nose. The only solace was that Father's increasing absences prevented him from witnessing every immoral spectacle. Somehow my homecoming and Ash's hedonistic explosion had coincided with Father's sudden disappearance. He was no longer home for dinner every night. In fact, some nights he didn't come home at all.

The stepmonster explained Father was staying overnight in town because of his work, and maybe that was true or maybe it was an excuse. What did I know? Father wasn't talking to me. His phone calls were relayed secondhand through an untrustworthy conductor. Tabitha could have reason to lie. Maybe Father was cheating on her. Maybe now that Tabitha was closing in on thirty she had lost her appeal and he was trading her in for a younger model. Maybe he wasn't that different from Ash after all. Maybe he was staying out late drinking or shacking up with another, younger version of Tabitha.

Our place in Lake Oswego was less than an hour outside Portland, but Father kept an apartment in the city, a condo in the Pearl District for nights he had to work late. I'd never been there, but he used to stay there a lot before Mother died. That all changed when he married Tabitha. Maybe it was because she was just nineteen and he didn't want to leave her alone, or didn't dare. Maybe he thought someone else—a neighbor, the pool boy, the UPS guy—would catch her eye if he wasn't there to keep her company. Whatever the cause, in the years since Mother's death, Father had come home nearly every single night. I guess that's what happens when middle-aged men marry teenagers, they have to watch their women a lot harder to make sure no Fabio-wannabe tennis instructor steals them away. It was also probably why Father hired our gardener, whose name I'd finally learned was Gualterio, even though Father insisted we call him Bob. He was about sixty years old, in the U.S. without papers, and probably poor as dirt, which I guess made Father feel comfortable Tabitha wouldn't run away with him.

Poor Bob, though, because he had to put up with Father's racist condescension and Ash's Caligula-style partying while he was just trying to keep the lawn mowed and shrubbery trimmed. Only that summer, I noticed that the grass seemed a little longer than usual and the topiary wasn't maintaining its customary definition. And every time I peeked out at Ash's wild poolside parties, I could see Bob lingering in the shadows, watching. I wondered what he was getting out of it, staring at all those young, supple bodies, watching the depraved debauchery playing out in the summer heat. I hoped he had someone to go home and share his hard-on with and he didn't just have to resort to beating off alone in the tool shed.

I stole another peek at the boys by the pool and noticed something surprising. The guys who'd been hanging around Ash all week weren't guys at all. They were women. Very masculine gals, to be sure, but girls, nonetheless. Having grown up in the Northwest, where even the straight women were utilitarian and capable of tossing eighty-pound bales of hay one-handed, it said a lot if someone's masculinity so overshadowed all visual cues to the contrary that I couldn't tell they were female-bodied.

But there they were, young women sporting swim trunks and T-shirts and the occasional ball cap. Of course, there were more feminine girls too, girls like Ash and a retro Bettie Page girl wearing a one piece, and a girl with glasses who wore surf shorts and stayed out of the water, lounging poolside with a fruity cocktail. Another girl wore a different color thong bikini every day, and a short girl with piercings in her lip, nose, belly button, and God knows where else, seemed to like having the details of her many tattoos slowly outlined by Ash's stray fingers.

Just like the men who preceded them, these women seemed to fawn over Ash, vying with each other to be the one to touch her, even casually. I watched the way their fingers brushed Ash's when they handed her a drink, the way they hoisted her on their shoulders for a game of chicken, or took their time rubbing sunscreen lotion on her legs, chest, belly.

It was odd to watch them compete for her attention. Ash seemed to choose a winner after a while, allowing only one girl to bring her drinks, pour sun-warmed pool water over her bronzed body, or light her cigarettes. But her fancy never lasted long. A few hours and the games began again, the competition for Ash's favor. Some brought her gifts. Others did dangerous dives, risking head injury in shallow water, or picked fights with each other. It was like watching *Wild Kingdom* during rutting season when the young bucks crashed their antlers together in a display of virility and an effort to court single does. Were humans driven by the same base instincts? Were the tens of thousands of years of evolution, the accomplishments of brilliant minds like Socrates and Shakespeare and Madame Curie thrown out the window when it came to sexual impulses and dating rituals?

A few of Ash's suitors seemed to rise above and differentiate themselves from the masses. One girl brought along a guitar and serenaded Ash with songs. I couldn't make out the words from my balcony, and I've never mastered lip reading, but it was pretty clear the singer was professing her undying love. Ash looked bemused. She received each of her subjects' pathetic adorations like her Royal Highness, sitting on her throne, deigning to bestow the slightest smirk to those that pleased her with their antics.

❖

The first time I witnessed it, the sheer shock of Ash fucking another girl in broad daylight threw me off my chair. My disgust was tangible. It made my skin crawl. Why was my sister so vulgar, so crass? For God sake! How come Ash never learned decorum like the rest of us?

That wasn't really fair. I *knew* she had been taught the rules of polite society. I'd seen Mother in action. So what drove Ash to violate all the tenets of good manners? It was revolting. But I couldn't turn away. It was like I *had* to watch. I had to pay silent witness to each surrender, see each woman throw her head back or bite her lip or cry out for more. I'd never made a lover respond with such enthusiasm. I'd never even experienced that kind of passion myself, let alone had that kind of sexual power, to bring a lover to their knees, to have them scream my name or beg for me not to stop.

I almost wished I could see more through my Peeping Tom glasses. I wanted to know what it was that Ash was actually doing, how her tongue flicked across that woman's clit, or how her fingers moved inside this other woman, to elicit such joyful responses. I wanted to be closer, to hear the words the women screamed in their moment of ecstasy. I imagined them as vivid verses, poetry that rivaled the love poems whispered by Sappho.

Watching Ash seemed to evoke the kind of stirring in my loins my college lovers never did. When I realized this, for a moment I was overcome with disgust at myself. What kind of pervert was I? That was my *sister*, for God sake! I suddenly saw Ash standing before me naked, and the image sapped the sexual arousal I'd been feeling. I threw down the sunglasses and vowed never, ever to watch again. I retreated to my room and my books. I decided to go cold turkey.

On my second day of detox, I started to feel like there was a physical struggle going on. I had to fight this force that drew me to the sliding glass door that led out to the balcony. I put all my muscles into it, sweating and straining, but my feet were being pulled out from under me. The balcony was a black hole and I was caught in the gravitational pull. I refused to give in. I vowed to ride this all the way through the pain of withdrawal even if it got as bad as *Trainspotting*. I had to conquer my addiction.

I realized I wasn't some kind of incestuous freak. When I watched Ash seduce those women I wasn't putting myself in *their* shoes. I didn't want to do Ash, I wanted to *be* Ash. When I watched, it was like I was the one down there by the pool, taking those women. I was no longer shy, bookish Megan. I was pleasing those women myself, wielding sexual prowess at seven feet deep. Freed of my moral dilemma, I gave myself permission to retrieve my binoculars and return to my post.

I realize, from an explicitly psychoanalytic viewpoint, that my voyeurism was a little like scopophilia, and there was something I lost by being a watcher instead of an actor. So it's not surprising that I eventually was drawn into the fray myself.

But back then I convinced myself that watching my sister wasn't that bad of a vice. After all, I wasn't drinking and driving, or doing drugs, or involving anyone else in *my* perversion. That made me feel morally superior to Ash and, at that point in my life, I'd do an awful lot to feel superior to Ash in any way. So I told myself I wasn't doing anything wrong. In fact, I convinced myself I was taking control of my sexuality. I was just imagining my way to erotic power, teaching myself sexual fluency, burrowing out of a prison of frigidity.

Sometimes I looked down at the naked bodies by the pool and discovered it wasn't just Ash making love with another woman. There was a whole group of them. Sometimes they were entwined into a ball of indistinguishable limbs, or they would take turns going one-on-one, with Ash kissing and stroking them, lying on the grass, or leading them back into the pool, clutching the sides of the deep end so that the passion wouldn't pull them under. I watched Ash's hands wander below the surface and the girls she was with, nay, the *women*, throw their heads back and open their mouths with silent moans or audible wails, or the same pleading sound that escaped my own lips and caught me off guard.

I don't know if Ash knew I was spying on her. She certainly never said so, not that we had a lot of conversations. Every once in a while I thought she was looking right at me, or I imagined she was winking at me, mid coitus, but most of the time I was pretty sure she was too caught up in the moment to be thinking about her twenty-two-year-old kid sister.

And I tried hard to remain unobtrusive, even more so after Cynthia began spending all of her time by our pool. Cynthia Newkirk was Ash's best friend, a lithe blonde with long hair and beautiful breasts. I'd first met her several summers earlier. Now I was discovering that Cynthia had a penchant for being topless nearly as often as Ash. Occasionally, Tabitha asked me to take mail from our main house out to the pool house for Ash, and I overheard her and Cynthia talking conquests, comparing sexual notes about their respective prowess.

It was pretty clear that Ash was the winner in any carnal competition, but I suspect Cynthia was trying to please her by offering as much titillation as possible, while secretly hoping to have Ash hanging on *her* every word just once, the way Cynthia and everyone else did whenever Ash opened her naturally perfect mouth. I had been forced to wear braces for three years, whereas Ash's forever-white teeth were straight from the moment they broke through her gums.

When Ash wasn't looking at Cynthia, I saw the way Cynthia's demeanor changed, the way she mooned over Ash like everyone else, absorbing every inch of Ash's body. Her longing glances lingered and her eyes flashed with jealousy whenever Ash paid attention to anyone else but her.

Cynthia's desire was so conspicuous I can still feel the

weight of it after all this time. It lurks there like an unfulfilled ghost doomed to wander the grounds until its hunger is satiated. It still lingers in the air around the pool house like a poisonous gas that, heavier than the air around it, clings to the ground years after it was released. When you step through the gaseous cloud, a sickly sweet aroma settles in the back of your gullet and makes you gag. You choke and claw at your throat as the gas robs you of oxygen and knocks you to your knees.

Poolside, each and every day seemed like Cancun's spring break, but back inside the main house, things couldn't have been more different. I could see almost the entire estate from my balcony on the second floor of the east wing. The pool to the left, the gardens to the right, and straight back between two carefully manicured hedges was Ash's pool house. I could even see *inside* the pool house as it was only shielded by two large, unencumbered French windowed doors.

As the summer passed by, I spent most of it in my bedroom, only emerging for a few hours in the morning and evening when I was required to join Father and the stepmonster in the dining room. Relations between Tabitha and me were as chilly as ever. At least she'd never tried to take Mother's place. But there had been a time, years ago, when Tabitha had tried to develop a relationship with me. She had grown up an only child and had these Pollyanna fantasies about what it'd be like to have sisters. I think that's why she wanted to be our friend.

Tabitha and Ash seemed to bond right away. Maybe I was a little jealous. Or maybe it was that way siblings have to differentiate themselves from each other, like if Ash was going to be best friends with Tabitha, then I sure as hell wasn't. I'm not sure what it was, but I hadn't wanted a relationship with Tabitha back then, and my utter rejection of her overtures created a sort of permafrost between us and prevented any potential affection from taking root.

With Ash banished to the pool house and Father staying at the office longer and longer hours, it seemed as though all the warmth had drained from the house. Stepping in from outside was like walking into an industrial grade freezer.

The house was ridiculously large for four people and their servants, and without Ash, it seemed cavernous and empty. I was always tempted to holler yodels down the long halls and time how long it took for the echoes to return, but it would have required a calendar instead of a stopwatch. I think there's some kind of mathematical equation for determining the expanse of an estate with echo technology, like the way you calculate the distance of lightning from the time between a strike and the sound of thunder.

I'll never understand why Father moved us out there in the first place. Maybe it was his way of grieving or a desire to protect us girls after Mother died, that had him relocate us to this huge estate in Lake Oswego, a Portland suburb with neither the color nor the potential dangers of the city. Even when all of us were home, most of the rooms in the palatial house remained empty, save for unused furniture shrouded in those protective sheets that make a place particularly haunted and frightening when you're a tween.

I remember Ash not being much help in that department. She thought it was hilarious to torment me, and she'd often disappear for hours at a time and then claim she'd been abducted by the ghosts of former residents who were all killed in a bloodbath murder-suicide perpetrated by an insane patriarch.

Even now, the rooms we used sporadically or merely passed through, like the sitting room, parlor, and formal dining room, remained untouched for weeks or months at a time—except by the maid staff, who were expected to clean every room at least once a week. My room was the size of a small apartment, and I had my own television set and refrigerator. For lunch all I had to do was call down and ask the cook to whip me up a sandwich. Mandated "family dinners"—how can it be a family dinner when Ash wasn't joining us?—at Casa Caulfield were quiet affairs.

Father seemed filled with rage when he was home, angrier than I'd ever seen him. Yet he never went out to the pool house and shut Ash down. I don't think he even attempted to talk with her once after kicking her out of the house. Ash could be annoying, but I don't understand why he didn't put his foot down, stop her debauchery, and bring her back inside. It was like he was waiting for her to change completely before he'd even acknowledge she still existed. They were both stubborn as mules and neither was willing to give an inch until the other gave a mile. I didn't realize it then, but she was begging for structure, not rebelling against it. I'll never understand why he didn't provide it.

Father was stone silent at meals, occasionally grumbling something under his breath that I couldn't decipher. But Tabitha seemed to understand because the comments usually sent her bursting into tears. I almost started feeling empathy for her. Here Father was pissed at Ash, and it was Tabitha and I having to bear the brunt of his anger. Behind closed doors, he and the stepmonster were fighting constantly. I guess with Ash out of the house they couldn't pin their anger on her so they were taking it out on each other.

That's why I was so surprised that Tabitha started joining Ash by the pool four weeks after I arrived, sunning and drinking and laughing. I'd never gotten along with Father's child bride, but she and Ash seemed to have some kind of understanding from the get-go. Being so close in age, I suppose they shared a certain perspective about the world. The age difference between Tabitha and Father had always perturbed me. I assumed Tabitha was a gold digger, in the relationship for Father's money. I never understood what it was about older men that some women found attractive. It always struck me as oddly incestuous wanting to date someone old enough to be your father.

I guess Ash saw it the other way around, like she felt it was inappropriate for Father to get involved with someone so young. For Ash, Tabitha's age seemed to make her a victim, someone too naïve to realize she was being used for her body.

Our different feelings about Tabitha were what first started driving the wedge between Ash and me. I couldn't forgive her for letting Tabitha take Mother's place, and Ash seemed to think I was being hypercritical and unfairly biased against Tabitha just because of her age.

Now they were hanging out together like a couple of best buds, and I couldn't understand how they could choose each other over Father. Wasn't that what they were doing? Surely when Father expelled Ash from the house it wasn't his intent for his wife to join the banished girl poolside. And Ash had always made it clear that she thought it was Father who took advantage of Tabitha, not the other way around.

I could see that Ash and I were never going to see eye to eye. We may have had moments when we were kids where we acted like friends. Chalk that up to us not knowing any better back then, and taking advantage of the convenience of in-home playmates. It was no longer convenient. There may have been parts of me that longed to be like Ash—or at least to have her self-confidence and sexual prowess, but I could see clearly that the two of us were never going to be friends. We were two very different people who'd been on divergent paths for far too many years to connect now. Otherwise, how could Ash spend that kind of time with Tabitha? Even worse, how could she let Tabitha hang on her words and follow her around like a lap dog, as if she was just another one of Ash's many lovers?

That was particularly disturbing.

Chapter Three

Ash was suddenly gone. She simply vanished. She was there when I went to sleep, but in the morning she never came out from the pool house. Cynthia and a handful of Ash's friends continued partying and lounging around the pool, but Ash never appeared. Making an excuse to drop by the cabana, I confirmed she wasn't there at all. Cynthia wouldn't—or couldn't—tell me where she was.

When I came back inside the house, Tabitha came out of her room, dark rings under her eyes, but a look of excitement on her face, which faded immediately at the sight of me. I wondered whom she was expecting.

"Oh, Megan," she said in disappointment. "You surprised me."

"Oh, sorry. Have you heard from Ash?" I quizzed, all the while knowing the answer. Tabitha dabbed the corner of her right eye with her pinky, the gentle swipe of her French manicure offsetting cobalt eyes. The motion made her look so delicate and unexpectedly precious, it stopped me in my tracks. That summer was the first time I noticed that Tabitha was a woman, not just a creature I called my stepmonster.

Tabitha had never been a mother to me. She tried, but by the time she married Father I was already a teen. I wasn't in the market for a new mother, and all of my adoration was occupied, having been heaped in equal parts upon Ash and Father, with little room for interlopers like Tabitha. In fact, I was threatened by her, this new authority figure that Father had supposedly rescued from poverty like a stray from the pound. I thought she wanted to replace my mother, and I wasn't willing to be mothered by anyone else, especially not a teenager. So I fought any affection she offered, assuming Father would eventually come to his senses and leave her. And though their marriage seemed rocky and forced at best, they never did split up.

But Tabitha had a look about her, like she was more a woman trapped than a woman rescued, and I had no idea why in this day and age she would stay married. Sure, there was a pre-nup, but those things don't always hold up in court and Tabitha was certainly still young and attractive enough to bag another wealthy suitor. If she left now. What was Tabitha holding out for?

"No. I'm worried about her." Tabitha broke my thought process with a quietly resigned admission. "Did you ask Cynthia?"

"Yeah, Cynthia doesn't know. She's useless. All of Ash's moocher friends are fucking useless. They don't really care about her."

Tabitha dabbed at her eyes again and covered her perfect pout with her hand so it looked like she was kissing her own knuckles. The move was self-protective, yet unexpectedly attractive.

"I know. I've told Ash that myself, but she won't listen." She tightened the belt around her silk kimono and walked to the French doors, peering out over the pool house and gardens. "Megan, do you love your sister?"

I turned, half expecting a lecture, when I saw tears streaming down Tabitha's face. My God, what the hell was going on here? "Of course I do. Why do you ask?"

She was mum again, her reasoning apparently snuffed out by emotion.

"Tabitha, is there something you want to tell me?" Had Father thrown Ash out? Had Ash moved without telling me?

Was Ash in jail? My mind was racing at this point, all with disastrous things that could have happened to my sister. As much as I envied her and competed with her, even at twenty-two, Ash was still my life, the person who completed me. Yes, she could still make me feel like a fourteen-year-old—hell, they all could, being home reduced me from a college grad to a sniveling teen all over again—but I couldn't imagine what I'd do if something had happened to her.

Her ash blond hair fell in front of her face as Tabitha dropped her head and sank down into a rouge leather armchair. Her lip looked like it was quivering, but there was no sound coming out, not even a breath.

"Tabitha? Did something happen to Ash?" I demanded, a bit louder this time. She was freaking me out.

"No, no, no," she said quietly. "I just wanted to, I just, oh, never mind. Everything's going to be fine." With that, she wiped her tears, pushed her hair back, and rose to her feet. The fragile flower I saw moments ago was gone, in its place the woman formerly known as my stepmonster, the bitchy beacon of suburban perfection.

I was stunned into silence. I couldn't help but feel torn at the display of emotion. It was as if I was seeing Tabitha—the inner Tabitha—for the first time, and the whole scene left me feeling…conflicted, I guess you could say. At a loss for words, I turned and went back to my room, where I spent the next several hours vacillating between reading—always my safe haven—and e-mailing my college friends. I was hoping a word from people who knew me as an adult would do more than just cheer me; it would add some buoyancy to my day-to-day existence. I wasn't sure why being home made me revert back to some self-doubting but petulant kid, but it did every time. Father wanted me here now and made it so I was trapped here until I could access my trust fund on my birthday. Who makes an inheritance due at twenty-three? All my friends got their money at twenty-one, or even eighteen. Still, the safety of what I knew and the security of Father's money trumped any desire I had to venture out on my own without a support system. As soon as my inheritance was accessible, though, I could leave this place and feel whole again.

Tabitha sulked and drank until Father came home. As usual, the two of them fought like cats and dogs, leaving me sitting alone at the family dinner table. I wanted to wait for them that night and ask about Ash, but I gave in to the coercion of my stomach and ate without them. I finished dessert and retired to my room. They were still locked in combat behind closed doors.

I stayed up late, waiting for Father to berate me for eating without him, but he never came upstairs. I was still awake when I noticed lights go on in the pool house. I was surprised by the intensity of the relief I felt that Ash was home again. I rushed to the balcony, only then realizing how worried I'd been about her unexplained absence.

The next morning Ash was gone again. She returned around noon, stayed for a few hours, and then slipped out again. At first I didn't even notice she'd left again until it struck me that there was something off with the way her friends were scattered around the pool. The configuration was all wrong. There were none of the clumping patterns that seemed to happen around Ash, like when you apply a magnet to the underside of a paper sprinkled with metal shavings. When Ash was by the pool, her admirers were equally drawn to her and they clustered around her, vying for her attention.

Over the next few days I confirmed that my deduction proved a fairly reliable indicator of Ash's presence or absence. I'd occasionally get it wrong, and Ash would emerge from the pool house after what I imagined was a quick shower or slow fuck. But mostly, my observations indicated that Ash was spending less and less time on the estate.

Following on the footsteps of Father's equally enigmatic disappearances, it was almost creepy. What was going to happen next? Was Tabitha going to start wandering off too? Where the hell were they going?

And what was up with Ash's friends? Did she give them permission to hang out when she wasn't there? Would Ash care to learn some of her suitors seemed to be coupling up when she wasn't around? What did they do behind the closed doors of the cabana? I mean, someone could damage or steal things. Just because Ash didn't care about anything didn't mean I should just let strangers come in and tear up the place. There could be heirlooms in there. The responsible thing, I decided, would be to check the place out and make sure nothing was missing or destroyed. Or perhaps I just wanted to snoop and any excuse would suffice.

Once I was inside the pool house I realized that I wouldn't be able to tell if anything was out of place. Nothing was the way I remembered it from the last time I was in there, when it actually served as a guesthouse for weekend visitors. Worse, I immediately felt like I was trespassing, like I'd broken the lock off Ash's diary, which I would never do. Well, maybe I'd have taken a peek if I stumbled onto one of the journals I had seen her writing over the years. You never know, they might have held the key to Ash's undeniable charm.

But I didn't find any journals that morning. I found a lot of empty alcohol bottles, sandwich baggies with a few leafless green sticks, expended whipped cream canisters, cigarette butts, and a sampling of lingerie strewn around the cottage. I looked for signs of foul play, but fifteen minutes ticked by like hours and I didn't find a pool of blood, deadly weapon, or dead body. There were no strange muddy footprints, broken lamps, or other signs of a struggle.

I was starting to worry about being caught red-handed. Things didn't turn out that well for me the last time Ash busted me for sneaking into her room. As the younger sibling I'd gotten stuck wearing a bunch of Ash's hand-me-downs. Tabitha insisted that Ash's clothing was far too expensive to discard when it was only "gently worn." It had to spend a season on my gangly frame before it was suitable for the Goodwill bin.

Ash and I were hardly the same size, so squeezing into her discarded and out-of-date fashions was a chore. I hated the clothing in my closet, the way it was two sizes too small and three years out of style. Just once I wanted to know what I'd look like in brand spanking new garments just in from Milan.

One time after Tabitha and Ash came home from shopping the *haute couture* of Portland's downtown boutiques—a trip I wasn't invited on—I snuck into Ash's room and pulled things out of her closet. Dresses that still had tags on them, shoes whose leather had never known the touch of soles, bags that were still packed with tissue. I piled them on the bed around me like wads of cash. I tried on her high heels and teetered around the room.

Then I spied the most beautiful black and white Chanel dress and had to try it on. I never had the bravery to be my sister, but I hoped somehow, maybe through fashion osmosis, that donning her chic outfits would make me just a little bit like her. I wanted to be as unassailable as she seemed. But I was also shorter and stockier than Ash, and as soon as I had the dress over my head I knew I was in trouble. I heard a seam start to tear and I was angling desperately to get out of the thing when I stood on one end, yanked the other, and found myself upside down on the floor, naked except for the gown covering my head.

"Ashley, did you—" Tabitha had come through the door, absentmindedly it seemed, before she realized that I was ass up on the carpet being suffocated by my sister's fancy new dress. "Oh dear God, Megan! What on earth are you doing?"

Did Tabitha think I had chosen to get myself caught up like that? I stumbled and stammered as she helped unhinge the dress from my head.

"Megan, I'm very disappointed in you."

I was always the kid who borrowed Ash's things, and I usually broke them. I never meant to. I just seemed to be far clumsier, more consuming than Ash was as a kid. It didn't matter. Neither Tabitha nor Ash ever let me live the episode down, and many times throughout our teens Ash would accuse me of wanting to be her. The worst part is, I could never deny that. But that didn't stop me from trying. Back then it felt like it would be a fate worse than death to have Ash know how desperately I wanted to be in her shoes. I was the ugly duckling, but I never woke up to be a beautiful swan.

Just before I sneaked out of the cabana I looked up at the tree-shrouded, vine-covered balcony that jutted out from my room. I got this creepy feeling like I was being watched. A wave of guilt washed over me. I wondered if this was how I'd made Ash feel. She must have known I'd been watching her all summer, living vicariously through her. I told myself it didn't matter. She probably didn't even mind. In fact, I bet she got a secret kick out of it. I got the feeling she liked having an audience. I definitely did not.

I slinked back to my room. I couldn't help but feel jealous that Ash could disappear at will, while I was stuck here with Mr. and Mrs. Angry-at-all-hours, my binocular sunglasses, and a constant fear that nobody would ever love me the way everyone loved my sister.

❖

I was bored and restless and tired of spending endless hours just waiting for Ash to come home so I could spend endless more spying at her and observing her world from my balcony. I knew I didn't have to be there, watching her, but I couldn't stop myself from wanting to see what it was like close-up. But every time I went down there and even attempted to talk with Ash, she dismissed me like some twelve-year-old hanger on. Still, I couldn't stop myself from trying again that morning. Since I could already see she was home, already in the pool half straddling an inner tube while floating in placid waters, I hoped the time was right for a heart-to-heart talk.

"Hiya, little sis," Ash crooned, sounding as flirty with me as she was with everyone else. "Coming down for a dip?"

I was caught off guard by how friendly and accommodating Ash sounded. It was as if she was never absent, as if we had never fought, as if Tabitha and Father weren't on the edge of divorce.

"I, yeah, why not. I'd love to just hang out and chat."

"Sure thing, Magpie."

Ash calling me by my childhood nickname threw me. Neither she nor Father had called me that since eighth grade. Clearly Ash was stoned or drunk or in therapy or something.

"I've been worried about you." Demanding to know where Ash had been was probably not the best tactic. "Where do you keep disappearing to?"

Ash looked taken aback. "I didn't know you cared, little sis." She smiled.

"Ashley, of course I care about you. Why can't we be like normal sisters, Ash? I feel like everyone wants to be with you, everyone is wrapped around your fingers, even Father and Tabitha."

A rather ominous chortle came from deep inside Ash. She sounded almost maniacal, and I couldn't tell if I was reading between the lines or if her cackle really was tinged with sadness.

"Magpie, you don't want my life. I've seen way too much. I've experienced way too much. I don't want this for you."

"What the fuck, Ash? Don't give me that seen too much bullshit! We're rich and spoiled and you're the queen of the castle here. You didn't even leave for college. You've spent your entire life in the state of Oregon. So don't act like you just spent six months fighting Vietcong or something."

"A minor in women's studies and the worst experience you could think of was war in Vietnam?" Ash laughed again, this time dismissively.

"You know what I mean." I had to smile myself, but I was still annoyed. Only Ash could be self-centered enough to think that even though she'd been the golden child, the spoiled one, Daddy's little girl, she'd had some kind of hard knock life. For God sakes, aside from her being the light of Father's eye and me going away to college, we'd had the same family, the same life, virtually the same everything, so how could she act like she had essentially been through more?

Ash smiled and pushed a swell of water up in the pool to splash me playfully. "It's too late for me to be the sister you deserve, Meg. I just don't have it in me. I am what I am and I don't think that'll be changing."

If I hadn't heard a bit of sorrow in her voice, I would have laughed at the Popeye-ness of her statement. Instead, it made me feel a little sad for Ash, if she was already resigned to the way things were at twenty-six. That didn't leave much room for growth. This was the first time we had spoken earnestly with each other, in a very, very long time, though, so I didn't want to challenge her too much. I just wanted to soak in the sun and my sister's luminosity and wish that things would stay between us exactly as they were at that very moment.

Chapter Four

They say nature abhors static conditions, so it's no surprise that nothing stays the same. Still, my prayers didn't go entirely unanswered. In the days that followed our conversation, it seemed like I'd had some kind of breakthrough with Ash and she'd remembered I was her kid sister, not some vile hanger on. She actually started inviting me down to the pool house, and she encouraged me to come hang out even when she was off on one of her wild adventures, the details of which she didn't divulge, but probably revolved around Ash and a bevy of female lovers pleasure fucking their way through Portland.

So there I was one night, sitting on the pool house's Ikea couch, watching Ash and Cynthia getting ready to go out, trying on dress after dress, throwing the discarded ones onto a growing pile of clothing scattered around the floor. Ash probably expected someone else to pick up after her. Maybe someone did. Looking around, I could see that the beer bottles and discarded drug paraphernalia I observed on one of my earlier visits were now nowhere to be found. I wondered if Ash had figured out a way to smuggle one of the maids in to clean the pool house or if one of her would-be lovers did that kind of dirty work. It puzzled me how we could have been raised in the same house and Ash had rich girl entitlement syndrome when I didn't. Or maybe she just didn't care. Maybe Ash was willing to live in squalor if no one else picked things up. I certainly didn't get it. But even as I felt annoyed by Ash's behavior, I wished somehow I could be included in even more of her world.

In that moment, she and Cynthia looked so happy and carefree, and I knew they were going out someplace exciting. I wanted so much to do something fun for a change, I asked if I could tag along.

"Oh, girl, you wouldn't last a minute with our crowd." Ash laughed.

"What do you mean?" I responded. "I've been hanging out with your friends for days."

"That's not the crowd I'm talking about," Ash snorted. "Besides, you could *never* keep up with us. You're still wearing a training bra, aren't you?"

My face burned and my witty retort died in my throat. The taunt felt needlessly cruel.

I couldn't keep up with Ash. She was four years older, had a faster engine under the hood, and was probably jacked up with nitrous oxide or whatever the sideshow crowd was pimping their rides with. In comparison, I was an old clunker running on the power of two horses.

If my darling sister hadn't always tried to hold me back and keep me from having any friends or sharing any fucking experiences, leaving me trapped at home with two people who had come to hate each other, then maybe things could have been different. Maybe I wouldn't always have come up short. Being held in comparison to Ash was kind of like using the same yardstick for Judy Blume and V. C. Andrews.

I was trapped in this second-class life and secondhand body and Ash didn't give a shit. She could have totally changed my life, just taking me with her one night and introducing me to the cool people. I'd seen plenty of uncool kids become totally hip just by extension of their cool siblings. I went to school with this one really unattractive chick who all the guys mooned over because somehow her class status made her pretty. Why couldn't

Ash lend me a little of her mojo? Why didn't she want to spend time with me? How could she be simultaneously full of self-confidence and then act like she was embarrassed to even be seen with me? Could I drag her down by my very presence?

Why did I bother coming home for the summer? I'd deluded myself into thinking we'd spend time together. Why did I imagine a miraculous change to our relationship? After ten years in the cold, what ever made me think Ash would invite me back in? Instead, we'd managed about fifty words since the beginning of the holidays, and that required battling Ash's fan club just to get close enough to speak.

"I'm not one of your minions, bitch." I muttered the insult under my breath and stomped off before Ash could see my lower lip trembling and my eye twitching, sure signs I'd be sobbing in a moment. No doubt she and Cynthia would get a laugh out of that.

Unable to reach my room before the dam burst, I stepped into one of our forgotten rooms and flopped down on the shrouded couch, full out sobbing. By the time my sobs had faded into sputtering hiccups, it finally dawned on me that Ash would always see me as a kid. It didn't matter that I was an adult, that I'd graduated college, that I was past the drinking age and had voted in my first elections. It didn't matter that I'd had lovers just like her, even though there hadn't been nearly as many and even though the world didn't fall at my feet, Ash would never see me as the grown woman I was.

An hour later, when I was all cried out, I slipped out of the room and was on my way to my room when I ran into Tabitha. She seemed so miserable it pulled me from my own dumps, and I actually tried being nice to her by striking up a friendly conversation about the Junior League, a frivolous topic that usually piqued her interest. But not tonight. She cut me off, shut me down.

My efforts to please others continued to go unnoticed. Why did I even bother? If I couldn't even get a woman I disliked to notice me, had I hit bottom? When would I stop needing others' approval? What would it take for me to feel like I'm enough just the way I am? Right as I was about to wallow in my own sense of failure, Tabitha offered me a tantalizing morsel.

"Your father's moving his stuff into one of the guest rooms." She pointed vaguely toward the west wing of the house.

I wondered what she had done to finally push Father to the point of leaving her. But why would he leave, instead of merely tossing her aside like he usually did with people who disappointed him?

Tabitha was teary eyed but sounded more resolved than I had ever heard, and I noticed a new sense of determination about her.

I wondered if I had misjudged her all these years. I loved Father, but even I could admit that he could be a bit of a chauvinist pig. I was making so much about being an adult, a grown woman, but wasn't part of that stepping out from under Father's shadow, being my own person and not just one of Father's lackeys? If I tried to step outside of myself and look at this objectively, didn't I have to acknowledge that Father had never seemed entirely kind or charitable to Tabitha? In fact, it was almost as though he had pitted her and Ash against each other in competition—for attention, affection, and just plain one-upmanship—for his own amusement. I could never stand the men who enjoyed dog fights, and I could see now that Father must have been a bastard to live with.

That summer I had been spying non-stop, not just on Ash and her ilk, but on Tabitha and Father, too. Their arguments were vociferous but never logical. I could never grasp what it was they were arguing about. "What happened?" I prodded, sure that Tabitha wouldn't tell me a thing.

"Megan, I'm not sure I could explain to you what's going on. More importantly, I think it's best you not know. Do know I'm not going anywhere."

What the hell? I was flummoxed by an admission that whatever had transpired was so complex it must be kept secret.

"Is Father leaving?"

"No. Nobody is going anywhere. Now I need to go speak with Ashley."

Of course she did. I'd noticed that Tabitha preferred to wait until I left before she joined Ash by the pool, bringing her cocktails and drugstore paperbacks like one of her flunky followers. It sickened me to see everyone so excited by Ash, even our parents. But then again, why wouldn't Tabitha, a woman Ash's age, want to hang out with Ash and her friends just as much as I did? There was something intoxicating about their endless party world. No doubt Tabitha gleaned from those meandering days that she had married too young, had given up too much of herself, had traded in the fun life for a man who was relatively distant, for life with a family that couldn't ever allow for the fun in dysfunctional. Maybe now she was going to have her quarter-life crisis and divorce Father.

The idea thrilled me, though I wasn't sure who I thought it would benefit.

Although I was certain it would be incredibly awkward and uncomfortable, I decided I had to go out and celebrate this new development, even if it meant going alone. Finding courage in having something, anything, change among my dreadful family dynamics, I resolved not only to go out by myself, but to go to a lesbian bar. Where to find one was a whole other story, of course, but I had the Internet on my phone and I was certain it couldn't be that difficult.

I should say this was not my first foray into a lesbian bar. Once, at college, I followed Terra to a queer dance club in the French Quarter where women danced with women and men danced with men and everyone was having a sweaty, debauched good time. I was starting to think maybe I was gay, not bisexual, not experimental, not a slut like Ash, just a plain old-fashioned lesbian. But the thing was I'd never known how to pick up other women, and I didn't know what I'd do if someone hit on me. The very thought made me so uncomfortable I could feel the sweat drip down my sides. Like, what if my junior high PE teacher showed up at the bar and tried to take me home? Or the wife of my old soccer coach, or even one of those slutty girls from porno movies? I wouldn't know what to do with any of those women. I didn't have a Brazilian wax, and I'd never strapped on a dildo, gone down on a girl, or owned a vibrator. I'd still only kissed two girls in my lifetime, including Terra, who frankly, did all the work in the sack.

Okay, I was in a little better stead now. At least I'd been *watching* the woman-on-woman erotic dance play itself out nearly every single day of the summer to this point, and I had a sense of what fervent sex looked like—from across the room. Surely that would help me in a real life situation where I was one of the players, wouldn't it? What if Andrea was right and I just sucked as a lover and I would never please another woman? Then where would I turn? Back to Mark and hairy, sweaty, don't-believe-the-G-spot-exists sex with men? I could actually feel the shudder crawl down my back. Perish the thought!

What I needed was an expert to come show me everything without asking for similar competence in return. I wondered how that worked. Andrea had talked about women who give other women pleasure but don't seem to want their lovers to reciprocate. I'd checked online for the terminology she used and found there was a whole sub-genre of "stone butch" lesbians who claimed they only derived pleasure from giving it, not receiving it, which sounded like a load of crap to me. But I liked the idea of someone pleasing me without wanting something in return, nonetheless. So I determined I should set out in search of a stone butch of my own.

It wasn't that I was afraid of the pussy. Okay, a little afraid. I'd read the myths in sociology about the *vagina dentata*, and while I knew my own furry creature wasn't fanged, how could

I be certain that was a universal truth, when so many cultures share these folk tales? Plus the pussy was just such a foreign and strange fruit and nobody had ever done mine justice, so how would I know what constituted "good"?

I wondered about Ash's lovers. They seemed awfully intent on pleasuring her even when she seemed like the aggressor, the top. Wait, what constituted a bottom, anyway? Was it only the person who got penetrated, the partner not in the leadership role? Or did it change, depending on who was being pleasured and who was doing the pleasuring? Did I need to understand these terms before I set foot in another lesbian nightclub?

I knew if I thought anymore about this, I was going to freak out and chicken out and end up spending another night alone in my room. Talk about pathetic. At least I'd get some research done, maybe answer a few more of my questions before tackling the real thing. Pa-the-tic. Then I figured out exactly what I needed. A shot of liquid courage. And I knew exactly where to find it. The latch on the liquor cabinet in Father's study had always been a little loose. Ash taught me years ago how to jimmy it open.

I helped myself to a shot of bourbon, and while it was still warming its way down my gullet, I marched back to my room and went online to check out the lesbian bars in Portland and found The Egyptian Club—apparently "affectionately known as the E Room"—on Division. That was a straight shot from the highway, and with a twenty-minute drive I'd have plenty of time along the way to prep. Or panic.

❖

"Ash!" I'd been at the club for fifteen minutes, nursing a five-dollar PBR in a velvet pleather booth while 90s music pulsated the walls around me, and I'd already heard that exclamation half a dozen times.

Since when did I look like my sister? Sober, no one had ever mistaken us, but maybe when someone was drunk enough that their ability to discriminate was lost and the world had turned a little blurry, maybe in that situation, I looked like my sister. I decided to level the playing field and over the next five minutes downed a couple more beers so that when the next woman grabbed me, happy to see my sister, I'd be ready to play along. That'd show Ash. I didn't need to tag around with her when I could *be* her.

"Yeah, baby?" I replied to the next siren call, and a pair of strong hands on my shoulders spun me around.

It made me a little light-headed. I giggled and put my arms out to stabilize myself and found my hands groping a butch-looking Filipino woman with short hair who was towering over me, her freckled face twisted into a glare.

"What the fuck are you doing here?" she spat in my face before my smile had a chance to fade. "Haven't you ruined enough lives?"

I was flummoxed by the allegation and quite honestly terrified. I'd never been in a bar brawl in my life, but I'd heard that fights could break out any minute in dive and dyke establishments, and I wasn't interested in being thrown through a plate glass window or having a bar stool busted over my head. My one and only fistfight happened my sophomore year of high school when Melissa McMichael sent me across the room with a quick right hook that broke my jaw, which had to be stapled shut for six weeks, during which time I lost all that unsightly baby fat. Come to think of it, without that broken jaw I may never have gotten a prom date. Still, I had no interest in experiencing fisticuffs again.

"I think you've me mistaken for someone else," I offered quietly. "I don't know you."

"You might not know me, Ashley, but I know you and you sure as fuck know my girlfriend, Kristy. You fucking tramp."

Damn. This was the kind of thing that could take all the fun out of impersonating Ash. I'd take the adoration, but I refused to be tormented for doing someone I didn't have the pleasure of doing. I hoped to calm the handsome stranger with rationality. "I'm sorry, I'm not Ashley. I'm her sister Megan—"

"Fuck you, you lying whore."

She was spitting mad. Her language was almost as filthy as Ash's. I was scared witless.

"You stole my girlfriend. Did you know that? She dumped me. We were going to get married next month until she just dumped me. She broke my heart. I couldn't work, I lost my job. I lost my fucking dignity. All because of you. You ruined everything."

"Look." I held my hands up in front of me, palms facing her, as though she could read them and know I spoke the truth. "I'm not Ashley, I swear. Want to see my ID?"

In response, the woman cocked her arm back and started to take a swing. Everything decelerated. It was as though we were characters in a slow motion fight sequence. Everyone stopped dancing and talking and they were all staring at us, waiting for that fist to connect with my jaw. A dozen thoughts raced through my head. *Duck. The first rule of fight club is: Don't talk about fight club. Do lesbian bar fights have the same rules? I don't want to drink from a straw again. If she breaks my nose, maybe the repair job will look better than the original. Who's Kristy and why did she leave this woman for Ash when Ash would never offer anything as tangible as marriage? What would Ash do if she were here? Would she even care that I'm about to be pummeled in a bar brawl because of her? What will Father say if I get arrested?*

Caught up in my own thoughts, I did nothing to prevent her fist from rearranging my face, when in a moment of uncharacteristic luck, her right hook was intercepted by a rather stunning but disheveled brunette, who repelled the fist, pushing it aside, while pulling me into an embrace. Even though we were in an impending bar brawl, being pinned against her taut body made mine prickle in places I didn't know had nerve endings.

The rest of the night was something I promised myself I

would record for posterity in my diary. I know that makes me sound like a giddy schoolgirl, but honestly, I felt like something wholly significant and amazing happened. Suddenly everything changed.

First, I was rescued from a certain beating by an enigmatic stranger and then Shane—that was my gallant rescuer's name— set me on the back of her motorcycle and we drove off into the sunset. Seriously, it happened just like a hokey Harlequin romance, except the knight in shining armor was a dyke in shining leather, and her mighty steed was a tricked-out Harley. Also, I wasn't much of a princess.

On the back of Shane's bike, the engine reverberated through my crotch and vibrated throughout my entire body until even my teeth were chattering along. To keep from falling off, I wrapped my arms tightly under her breasts and held on for dear life. The ride was exciting enough. I could have stayed behind her on that bike for hours, but before I knew it we were at a park fumbling around in the darkness.

I felt a bit foolish at first, until we smoked a bowl of weed, and soon we were lying in each other's arms on the banks of Lake Oswego, talking and kissing for so long that we were still there hours later when the sun began to rise.

Everything about Shane was fascinating. She was beautiful and smart and dark and sarcastic. A poet and performance artist with a rebellious streak and a sensitive side. Shane's mother and father, both drug addicts, split when she was two. She bounced back and forth between them until running away at fourteen. She'd been on her own since then, sometimes selling drugs to get by. She'd had a number of lovers but never a real girlfriend. Her number one goal in life, she said, was to find true love.

I'm not sure if I was a sucker for a romantic story or if it was just the rush of feelings from that evening, but I wanted Shane so badly. She waited for me, just talking, drawing me out, never making a move until I was practically begging for it. After a couple of hours of talk, my body was just aching for that first kiss, and by the time I leaned in for it, I wanted to explode. The kiss was warm, soft, wet, unforgiving. I melted into it as though Shane was a part of me, and before I knew it I had taken her hand and shoved it inside my panties. I was wet and full and she parted me with her fingers like a locksmith with a deadbolt. She was in and out of my cunt, twisting me up in passion before I could think, and soon her head was down there too, her tongue lapping at the sides of my clit, teasing me for what seemed like hours before giving in to my desire. I couldn't wait for her though. I tore at my own shirt, pulling my bra straps aside and pointing my nipples into the early morning air. I would have lapped them up myself if my tongue could reach, but instead I used my fingers to twist and massage them while Shane licked and lapped, all the while still moving her hand in and out of me.

Just thinking about it in retrospect makes me want to orgasm like I did that night, over and over, each time crying out and pushing her back, unsure whether I could take yet another *la petite mort*.

It was nearing sunup when we finished, too exhausted to go on but still eager for each other's bodies. Shane wanted me to come back to her place, but I couldn't. I already knew I'd incur Father's wrath over our mandatory "family" breakfast by staying out all night, and suddenly I felt awkwardness too. A bit of embarrassment at having let this relative stranger inside me so much, literally and metaphorically. As my body was flushed and weak, almost heightened from being stimulated for hours, my mind was racing with a mixture of emotions—excitement and guilt tops among them. I had Shane rush me back to my car in hopes I could make it back to the estate before Father was up for his usual coffee, half grapefruit, and *Wall Street Journal* breakfast ritual.

I was successful, to a point. When I got to the house, I ran to the door and discovered the house was still relatively dark. Unfortunately, my keys were missing. My whole bag was missing, actually. Thinking I left it at the lake, I began looking for some other way to get into the house without alerting the inhabitants. I tried the other doors, the windows, even the back gate, all of which were locked. Probably because Father is a security freak who thinks people are trying to steal our stuff at all times. Fortunately, as I started to hunch down by the front door, frustration welling up in the corner of my eyes, Maria opened the door.

"Oh, Miss Caulfield, you scare me," Maria said in startled, broken English. "Are you all right?"

"Oh, yes, yes, I just got locked out and didn't want to wake anyone. Is Father up?"

"No, Señor Caulfield has not risen today. I'm preparing breakfast." She pointed to the newspaper on the stoop. Of course, Father doesn't even get his own newspaper off the porch.

"Great. Let's keep this between us." I grabbed her and pecked her cheek, an impulsive thank you for keeping my secret.

Maria seemed bemused. She probably knew what a hard-ass Father could be more than anyone.

❖

Flush with my sexual conquest, I put on my bikini and marched down to the pool. Screw Cynthia and Ash, I thought. It was my pool, too. I wasn't going to let our spat the other day force me back into the imprisonment of the house. I didn't need Ash's invitation or permission, not that day, not when I was emboldened by my night of passion.

Ash and her friends were already out by the pool. Their conversation went from a loud chatter to hushed whispers. Geesh, she couldn't even share a fucking conversation with me? God, some days I hated my sister.

I ignored them, spreading my towel out across one of the lounges before massaging some sunscreen onto my skin. I finally muttered my hellos a few minutes later, while I was dipping my toes in the surprisingly cold water. Normally I'd spend a half hour slowly wading in deeper and deeper, gradually getting used to the temperature, but not that day. I tossed a pool mattress in the water, held my breath and dove in. It was shocking. Any element of sophistication I might have displayed was quickly undermined by my ungainly struggles to board the floatation device. Every time I'd capture it and try to shove it under my ass, I would end up falling over backward splashing and sputtering while the mattress popped up on the other side of me, rising like a missile from the water. I finally managed to flop my body onto the float with all the gracefulness of a sea lion flinging itself onto a dock. I lay there panting, so loud that I almost drowned out the commotion of Ash yelling over my head at some newcomer. My back was to the gate and I didn't even bother turning to look at what was sure to be another of Ash's conquests—why would I care who she's whoring around with now? But I couldn't help overhear her tantrum.

"What do you think you're doing here?" Ash was practically yelling. "I told you I don't want to see you again. I can't believe you've come to my home."

"But—"

"No buts, a no is a no, you got that?"

"It's not what you think. I'm here for Megan."

Ash cut the woman off again, but this time the voice had a tint of familiarity to it so I swirled around on my pool mattress just in time to see Shane standing there, red-faced, holding my purse.

Damn. For some reason it had never occurred to me that even my one-night stand might know Ash. It was a crushing blow. My knight in shining armor had already been her knight, had already been in her. I was always second, never number one. Maybe that's why Shane had noticed me, what she'd liked about me, what attracted her to me, my resemblance to Ash, however slight. Oh, my God, what if she was just with me because Ash told her no and I was as close as she could get to the real thing?

I felt the heat flushing my cheeks and wanted to disappear.

I was frozen in place, afraid to move for fear I'd catapult myself back into the water. Then I could feel all eyes on me and I decided maybe that wasn't such a bad idea. In fact, I wished I could just melt right there like the wicked witch of the *Wizard of Oz*. As a liquid I'd run right off the mattress and become indistinguishable from the water around me. Before I could process it all though, Shane shoved my handbag at Ash and turned and ran.

"Wait, Shane!" I shouted, trying gallantly to go after her but instead just falling off my float and ruining whatever decorum I had left. By the time I swam out of the pool, climbing up the stairs at the shallow end and bridling at Ash's malevolent demeanor, Shane had sped off on her bike and I was livid.

"You cunt!" I yelled at Ash. Perhaps the first time in my life I had called another woman by that name. It seemed the most apt that day. "I can't believe you think everyone is here for you. What a freakin' narcissist you are. Just because you can fill this pool with your toadies, mostly because you're such a whore, doesn't mean the world revolves around you, Ashley!"

I drew out the name like it was two different words: Ash Lee. I knew she hated her given name, long abandoning it in favor of the androgynous Ash, her favorite character from a movie, too. Calling her a whore wouldn't bother her, but calling her by her girlish name might.

"Listen, child, don't kid yourself. Shane is sloppy seconds, babes. She's only with you because she can't have me."

My hand flew at her face as though on its own accord. I watched it slap her across the cheek and was certain that the shock in her eyes was mirrored in my own. I had never before raised my fist to her, and I was as surprised as she was by my reaction.

Ash had quick reflexes and she caught my hand by the wrist before I could pull it away. "Damn, Magpie," she sneered, using my childhood nickname to patronize me. "You want her so bad, you can have her. Shane's a loser dope fiend I sent packing. You want my rejects, kiddo, you go right ahead."

"Fuck you, Ashley. Maybe you were just her practice round,"

I shouted, yanking my arm from her grip. "Shane likes me for me, not me because I look like you!"

"You trying to convince me or yourself?" Her words cut me with their accuracy.

But I was like a runaway train and I couldn't stop. "And we both know I sure as shit don't act like you."

"Whatever." Ash drew the word out into additional syllables. She was so blithe. Her nonchalance infuriated me and I wanted to strike out physically. But Ash had just volleyed back demeaning one-offs, as though I wasn't even worth a full argument. And though her cheek was bright red where I'd slapped her, and it must have stung, she hadn't even flinched. Something about that frightened me.

Suddenly I was biting back tears. I didn't want to give her the satisfaction of seeing me cry, so I snatched my purse from her hands and dashed off headed toward the house.

"I wonder if she fucks like you?" I heard Cynthia say as I rushed past.

Ash laughed. "Wouldn't you like to know?"

They both cackled like hens as I darted out of earshot.

CHAPTER FIVE

I no longer cared about my sister and her little sex games. I had my own play toy in the dark, foreboding Shane. We started rendezvousing more and more, sometimes at her apartment in the city, other times at the estate, hidden in the east wing where Father and Tabitha couldn't hear. Each encounter left me breathless in anticipation for the next.

"What's this one?" I was playing connect the scars on her body, languishing over every line, every mark.

"I was playing flag football and ran into a rake."

"And this one? Let me guess, knife fight?"

"Yeah, with a cantaloupe." Shane laughed, a hearty, guttural guffaw I found intoxicating.

"It's my turn," she said abruptly, flipping me over and crawling on top of me. "I want to play connect the dots on your body now."

I did like the sound of that, but I was barely comfortable with my naked body during sex, much less so during a game of map my flaws. "I'm not sure I have as many things to connect."

Would that stop her?

"Well, let's make it interesting then," she said, tugging off the remainder of my clothes. "You close your eyes. When I get to something, you have to tell me where the mark came from."

"Okay," I drawled, uncertain.

"Oh, there's one catch." I waited, already enticed but nervous nonetheless. "I'm only going to use my tongue."

I felt myself getting wetter already. Just the thought of Shane's tongue rolling up and down my body, darting in and out of crevices, demanding to know them, made me feel weak kneed and light headed. I'm pretty sure my legs parted right then and there, but Shane made a point of blindfolding me and laying my arms to the sides of my body instead of using them to cover the pooch on my stomach or my hairy triangle or some other place I would normally try to hide from insecurity.

"No touching, missy," Shane said. She began slowly, one finger at a time, using her tongue to trace and then point at a spot between my thumb and forefinger.

"What's this one?"

"My grandmother was pointing with a knife in the kitchen and my hand hit it."

"Ew, painful." She moved on up and down each finger to my wrist to the inside of my elbow, using her tongue to stroke the inside and then the outside. "And this one?" Her query was muffled from sucking on my elbow, a motion that I was finding almost intolerable in its excitement.

"Uh, I don't know…" I trailed off moving my hand to her face and trying to push her down.

"No shortcuts and no hands, I said." Shane played back with me. She knew how badly I wanted her inside me, on me, down there now, but she was drawing it out. My stomach knotted, desire like a clenched fist in my gut.

"What's this one?" she demanded again.

"Oh God, c'mon! Bobby Jenson pushed me off my bike in fourth grade." All the blood in my body had rushed to my cunt, which was now so wet I could barely keep my legs together without matting. "Move!"

Shane was controlled though, surely enjoying this little game. She moved from the elbow to my shoulder, under my arm and on to my neck. Finding no birthmarks or blemishes of any sort, Shane bit my neck slightly, in a sort of modified hickey. It left me speechless. I moved my own hand down to my crotch. I couldn't wait anymore. I would please myself if I had to.

But Shane caught me and pinned the wayward hand down with hers. She grabbed my other hand and when I couldn't bear it anymore she pinned it too, now using just her mouth to lick and nibble every single inch of my body from head to toe. The questions had ceased on her end, but the curiosity was still there, I could tell. When she flipped me over onto my belly I considered dry humping the bed, except, well, it could hardly be called dry humping with the state of delirium I was in.

"Shane, please." I was beyond begging. Her tongue had hit every trigger point, every erogenous zone on my body except the big one, and I wasn't sure I could handle any more stimulation.

"Yes, dear," Shane whispered in my ear.

"Please do it. I need you. Now."

Before I could beg anymore, Shane forced my legs apart and from behind rammed her tongue in my cunt. She thrust it forcefully in and out of me, flicking along my clit with each new shove. As greedy and demanding as her tongue seemed, it propelled me to orgasm within minutes. But Shane wasn't ready to stop there.

As I lay spent on my bed, hoping to God nobody heard me shriek when I came, Shane shuffled about the room and came back with a purple marbled dildo that looked alarmingly like a boomerang. I wasn't sure what we would do with it, but I didn't want her to be aware of my naivety.

"Wait, let's rest a minute," I stalled.

"Shhh, trust me."

And so I did, lying back again while Shane gently moved one end of the lubed-up contraption inside me and placed the smaller end inside herself. She began rocking back and forth, her hips jutting out at me at random angles, our pubic hair soon matted and entwined like a natty old wig. I quickly learned that Shane could wield this double-headed dildo as surely as my college fling, Terra Moscowitz, strapped hers on. And with this I saw the desire and pleasure inside Shane as every time I pushed back, the toy throbbed inside of her. I could tease her now. I could hold back, slow down, then speed up, using my hips and my pelvis to control everything.

I entwined my fingers with hers and pushed our arms above our heads so Shane's whole torso fell onto mine. Her tits moving on top of mine, her mouth next to my neck, it was all too much, and I could barely contain myself until Shane started quivering. Her legs were shaking now, ferociously trying to control her body, but one final thrust and her back arched and she let out a loud, animalistic howl. I let myself orgasm too finally, collapsing into her again.

When I awoke an hour later I knew I had to get Shane out of there before Father caught wind of us. I thanked God for this ridiculously large house. I ushered Shane out to the street and made my way back to the exit by the servant's quarters. And who was standing there but my sister.

"Ashley! Oh, my God. You scared me."

"Maybe that's your guilt talking."

"Shut the fuck up. I don't know what your problem is." Ash had picked a crap time to pretend to care about me. I wasn't buying her argument that Shane was using me to get to her. "And how exactly does her having sex with me get to you, hmm? Don't try to play big sister with me. You haven't acted like my sister in a long fucking time."

"Look, I'm trying to stop you from getting hurt, kiddo. Shane's no good, she'll just break your heart."

"You know what? I'm pretty damn sick of you trying to get me going over this. I know for a fact that Shane doesn't want your skanky ass. She's in love with me."

Ash was silent for a moment then she smiled, a glint in her eye. "All right. Don't say I didn't warn you. I just thought it would be nice for you if you didn't have to have my discards all the time."

Enough was enough. I pounced on Ash like a tiger cub, pushing her to the ground, kicking and screaming. Before she knew what hit her, I had a clump of her hair in my hand and I was pushing her face against the ground.

"I have had enough!" I screamed. "Stop fucking with me!" I yelled each word as though it were its own proclamation. I was filled with rage and venom and years of disappointment at our relationship. This was the final blowout we had been coming to for years. She was a shitty sister, a crappy harlot who didn't care about anyone but herself.

When I realized she wasn't fighting back but was instead lying there laughing I realized the futility of my anger. Something about Ash wasn't right, that's just the bottom line. Taking her down, literally, in the garden in the middle of the night wasn't going to change that. I stood up, dusting myself off before walking away.

"You know, Ash, I don't know why you have to ruin this for me. Why can't I have one girl who wants me when you so clearly have dozens?"

I didn't wait for her reply.

❖

Years ago I used to love charity galas. The ball gowns, the fancy hors d'oeuvres, the way everyone treated my family like royalty. But at the Care for Kids Charity Gala in July, I was sitting at a table in a stupid chiffon dress that made me look like a chubby sorbet, wishing I were with Shane, at her apartment, smoking dope and watching *Three's Company* reruns. But I didn't have a choice. Apparently Ash didn't either because she was there too, as was Father. We were all together like old times, like we were a family, we were there watching my stepmonster receive an award for her charity work, aka spending Father's money to do good. I didn't know what the big deal was. It's not like she had to do anything except write a check, but apparently that check was big enough to earn top nods for saving the children or feeding the children or some sort of verbiage about children. I wondered if the people who actually did the labor involved with the charity's work resented her getting this award when they toiled in anonymity. God forbid the wealthy dirty more than their index finger.

Tabitha was flitting around the place, shaking hands and smiling at everyone, and Ash was at her side. They kept exchanging glances like they shared some kind of secret. The thought affected me. What kind of secrets could Ash and Tabitha share? I wanted to march over there and interrupt their reverie with my presence so that I stopped feeling like I was outside looking in. But they looked too insular, too serene and self-protected. This was clearly their element, not mine and not Father's. Just what kind of secret did the two share? What did they know that I didn't?

Father was in the corner, but I could see he was watching them too, scowling as well. He looked as unhappy as Tabitha and Ash looked happy. And me, well, I'll bet I had a scowl too, though I was trying to suck it up and get the night over with.

From my corner of the room I could see Ash go back to the bar again and again. She'd had at least half a dozen martinis, best that I could tell, a quantity that would have me under the table by then. But for Ash, she just seemed louder and happier than she was at the outset. When toasts started ringing out from friends and well-wishers, I was hoping it meant the gala was starting to wind down. The silent auction was over. They were clearing the bar. The awards had been had. The deejay had shut down. Soon I could go home and call Shane.

But instead, Ash decided to toast the stepmonster, this time offering accolades at the top of her lungs. "You have an amazing fundraising acumen," Ash said, way too loudly as Tabitha tugged on her dress and smiled at the ground. "Congratulations on being such a ball-breaker when it comes to money."

The crowd offered up nervous laughter. Was it a joke? Should they laugh? Nobody knew. Not even me.

"And for marrying well. And for loving all us perverts out there. Right, Daddy-O?"

The crowd was astounded by Ash's proclamations and all eyes turned from her and Tabitha to Father, whose fists were balled in anger as he stormed off. Ash walked off in a different direction, leaving me standing next to Tabitha, who attempted to regain some dignity in the moment.

"Well, who said booze and speeches don't mix?" The crowd around her laughed, partly out of anxiety, partly due to their alcohol consumption, but mostly just for the chance to wash themselves of the very public private spectacle of my family.

Tabitha grabbed my elbow gently and whispered in my ear. "Megan, I'm worried about your sister. I think she's using drugs, real drugs, not just marijuana. I think it's all Cynthia's fault. That girl is trouble."

Suddenly, I was less angry at Ash and more worried about her. What on earth would make her lose it in a crowd like this? The old Ash, the person I knew years ago, before I went off to college, she used to worry about what people thought of her, what others said about her. She worried about where she was going in life and who she would become. And as stupid as our stepmother was, this seemed like something Tabitha got right. Ash did seem more and more troubled lately. She seemed to have no compass in life—moral or otherwise—and she was floundering.

Some sick part of me was secretly pleased.

"Can you talk with her?" Tabitha was teary eyed.

"Of course." I meant it too. I loved my sister. I did. I just hated who she'd become as of late. And while I felt like it was she who owed me an apology and should reach out first, I was willing to be the bigger person and offer her an olive branch. Maybe if I could put an end to this sibling feud we could bridge the chasm between us and relate to one another like normal sisters.

❖

Since Tabitha was the night's woman of honor, she and I were stuck at the party another few hours. How Father and Ash got home I'm not sure, but when it was time to go, the two of us rode back in the Bentley alone.

"You looked happy there tonight," I said, hoping to find out what was really going on behind the scenes. When Tabitha only smiled I tried a different tack. "You and Father didn't seem to spend much time together, though."

She turned, cocking her head as if she were evaluating how frank she could be, and smiled again. "You know your father doesn't enjoy these types of outings. Just because I'm happy doing charity work doesn't mean he is."

It was a simple statement but one that felt loaded with emotional information.

"Why do you stay?" I prodded. Maybe she was sad and drunk enough to answer honestly.

"What?"

"Why do you stay married to Father? Is it the money?"

Tabitha paused, reflectively, her eyes glistening again like they did after Ash's outburst. She was pensive and thoughtful and though she was crying now, she was still quite beautiful. What did she see in Father, a man thirty years her senior?

"Megan, I'm not sure you could understand the nuances of my marriage." She looked faint and stricken. Perhaps I touched a nerve. "It's hard to explain why we do the things we do, but you must know I'm not some simple ninny pining away for a cold and distant workaholic husband."

I wanted to be frank with her, too. "Well, that's certainly how it looks from the outside sometimes."

"You of all people should know looks can be deceiving."

"What's that supposed to mean?" I felt confrontational and defensive.

"Nothing, dear, I just mean, what you see isn't all there is in any situation."

As soon as we arrived home I rushed straight to the pool

house to talk with Ash about this strange conversation. Out of the corner of my eye, I caught sight of Shane's bike and immediately felt flush with anticipation. Being with Shane would make this whole night so much more palatable. I hastened toward the bike to find her first. She was probably waiting by the pool for me, I figured. But when I couldn't find her there I continued on to the pool house in case she was chatting with Ash.

I didn't even stop to knock in my rush of excitement, but I'll forever wish that I did. Inside, Ash lay supine, her undulating legs wrapped around Cynthia's neck, while Shane was nuzzled up against Ash. It's hard to say which is worse: finding your girlfriend making it with your sister or finding your girlfriend in a threesome. But certainly finding both of those things at once when you spent the whole night dreaming about the bitch is among life's worst moments.

I was instantly enraged and violently nauseous, and while Cynthia barely recognized my presence, Ash sat up and said, "Come in, little sister," in her most flirtatious tone.

The whole sight of it made me sick to my stomach. I stood there, an exclamation barely forcing its way up my throat and out my mouth, as I registered real disbelief.

"Wait, Megan, I can explain," Shane began as I shook my head violently.

At that moment I didn't know whether to be angry or disgusted, and if it was anger I should feel, who deserved my wrath the most. Was my sister right all along? Was this her fucked-up way of showing me that Shane was just using me to get to her? Or did Ash declare war, seducing Shane just to hurt me? What had I ever done to deserve this?

The moment seemed frozen in time, but silent admonition turned to pure bile.

"I hate you. I hate all of you!" I cried as Shane rushed toward me. "Don't you ever fucking touch me again! And you, you…" I pointed at Ash, who seemed too drugged up to even care that I was yelling at her. God, what was wrong with her? What a horrible human being. "I wish I could be like you, Ashley—all tits and ass and cold and dead inside. I don't know what's wrong with you, but you're toxic. I don't want anything to do with either of you ever again. You deserve each other."

As I ran out the door I could hear Ash say something but couldn't decipher it. For all I know she was laughing.

CHAPTER SIX

I spent the next two weeks inside the house where tensions seemed to escalate as well. My father and Tabitha seemed to be yelling at each other constantly, both of them drunk off their asses. The air around the whole estate felt pregnant with disaster. I didn't know what was going to happen, I just had that terribly foreboding sense that something had to give. I just hoped I would be okay in the wake of whatever storm was brewing.

Tabitha and Father lived in different rooms now, the three of us eating solo in the kitchen by turn. Maria had learned to make my favorite comfort foods: grilled cheese, mac and cheese, cheesecake. Without Shane, I turned into a pudgy cheese-freak. We hadn't talked since that horrible night in the pool house. She never called me again, not even an attempt at an apology. Even worse, I'd seen her out at the pool with Ash and Cynthia. The three of them, skanking around like whores.

I couldn't bear to watch it anymore. I kept my shades drawn at all times, squirreling myself away in my novels, reading one after another, cramming my head full of words and other people's lives so I wouldn't have even a second to dwell on my own miserable one.

I desperately needed to get out of this place. Maybe I'd go to grad school or spend a year backpacking across Europe like my college roommate. I didn't know, maybe getting a job and moving to the city would be good. I just wanted to do something to get away from my whole family. They were all nuts.

The only problem with the options I came up with was that they all required some kind of planning. And I couldn't find the energy to do any of it—not searching job ads, not filling out graduate school admission applications, not even shopping for backpacking gear. I felt tired all the time; I ached all over; I burst into tears every few minutes.

Maybe I should just go on vacation somewhere far away, somewhere like Florida or the Cayman Islands, somewhere with frozen tropical drinks that could help me forget—everything. Somewhere I could get my head together and figure out what to do with my life. If only I could get Daddy dearest to loosen the purse strings so I could book a flight immediately.

In all these years I'd never even had a credit card in my own name. I wasn't an adult. I was a child. A foolish, gullible child so desperate for love she couldn't even tell when she was being used. I thought Tabitha was stupid, but at least she seemed to know exactly what she was exchanging for what.

The putter of a small engine pulled me from my thoughts. I envisioned Shane's motorcycle coming up our drive, and I couldn't help but reminisce about her touch on me, her whole effect on me. Shane was my first real lover—not just those college kids and the few tumbles in dorm room beds. She was the first person I'd ever said the L-word to. But now I couldn't stop imagining Ash and Shane together. Every time we were together, was Shane imagining I was Ash? Ash was probably right. It was better to use people than to be used by them.

I was going to change my life. I was never going to let someone get that close to me again. I resolved to begin my new sentimentality-free life in the morning. I dozed off fantasizing about how great it would be to be aloof and in control.

Although I was never much of a television junkie, my secret vice was falling asleep to the sound of crime shows playing in the background. *Law & Order*, *CSI*, if it had cops, I could fall asleep to it. I'm not sure what it said about me that nothing lulled me to sleep like the noise of sirens, running feet, and gunfire. I think I can blame it on Mother, who used to read Edgar Allan Poe aloud as bedtime stories: "The Tell-Tale Heart," "The Pit and the Pendulum." I don't know why. I guess there's something twisted in our genes.

So it didn't shock me when I heard the scream. I assumed it was the television, that the sleep timer hadn't clicked in and turned it off yet, but then, just before I closed my eyes again, I realized that the room was dark. Pitch black. There was no telltale glow from the television. I looked up and discovered the set wasn't on. Something was wrong.

I jumped up and something pulled me to the sliding glass doors that led to my balcony. I shoved aside the heavy curtains just in time to witness some sort of flash of light. Was that someone disappearing into the trees? Was that a scream, or maybe just a gunning engine? My heart jumped at the thought of Shane's motorcycle, and as pathetic as it was, I immediately searched for her bike. It wasn't there.

Could she have left that quickly? Was I wrong in thinking I'd heard the distinct sound of a motorcycle? I stood on the balcony for a moment, sweeping my eyes across the estate, seeking anything that might have caused the noise. I found nothing. Maybe Ash had her TV turned up really loud. I listened intently for the sound to repeat. It didn't. There was no backfiring car, no late night foray on a golf cart, no landscaper firing up a chainsaw for midnight pruning, nothing.

I realized that everything had gone still. Even the crickets had stopped chirping and fallen silent. I looked down at the pool house, checking for the flashing lights of Ash's television, but it was dark. I couldn't tell if there was a problem, but an ominous sense of foreboding washed over me. Something was wrong. Something was wrong with the night air. It was too quiet.

And then it wasn't. I heard yelling, doors slamming, feet pounding hard against the ground, people running this way—

toward the pool house. Toward Ash. Something was very wrong. Flashlights bobbed closer and the voices resolved and I heard Father's husky voice howling out Ash's name.

I almost jumped. I almost dove right off the balcony because that would have been the fastest way down, the quickest method to reach the ground. *Oh, my God—Ash!* I didn't pause to speculate on what was wrong, I didn't waste any time stitching together my darkest fears. In that moment I didn't remember any of the terrible things Ash had done lately, the things that had made me hate her, not even what she had done with Shane—none of it. In that instant all of that was gone. I just ran. I flew out of my room without even bothering to throw on a robe or slippers.

I took the stairs three at a time, landing hard on a bent ankle and not even flinching at the pain. The front door stood open. The sinking feeling in my stomach plummeted with all the force of an out of control elevator plunging a hundred floors.

There was something incredibly disturbing about the sight of a home's front doors gaping wide open. There was almost a perversity to it, and I wanted to look away, to shield my eyes from the obscenity.

I thought of Ash. The image of her face in my mind was enough to block out the doors as I sprinted through them and down the path. The ground was cold and damp under my bare feet. I've always had sensitive feet, and normally I couldn't stand to go barefoot unless I was walking in weathered beach sand. When forced to, I'd have to hobble slowly along, grimacing at every step, as though I were walking over hot coals. But that night I didn't even slow down.

As soon as I hit the ground I could see that the French doors to the pool house were wide open and all the lights turned on. I could hear someone wailing, or was it a dog howling? It didn't seem real, didn't seem possible that the sound I was hearing could be coming from a person. Silhouetted against harsh lights of the exposed pool house, I could see figures hunched and bent over. As I got closer, I could see there was something heaped on the floor in front of them, a pile of some kind.

I ran faster. I could hear the sound of the surf pounding in my ears. Was that my pulse? I ran. One of the figures swept the pile into their arms and stood up. The heap unfolded into the shape of a person.

I froze. The shape didn't stand up on its own. Its feet didn't touch the ground. It just hung there in the air as limp as a rag doll. I heard someone scream, "No!" and the sound echoed off the canyons in my ears. It wasn't until Gualterio called my name that I realized I was the one shrieking. As though released from a spell, I started forward again. Just as I did, I sent a prayer Heavenward. I begged the man upstairs for something I will always be ashamed of. *Please God*, I thought, *don't let it be Shane.*

Almost immediately I knew my prayer had been answered. I could make everyone out. Tabitha was wailing, holding Ash's limp, bloody body in her arms. Maria was sobbing and crossing herself while Gualterio and Father were huddled together as though conferring. Father was shouting something I couldn't decipher. A distant police siren rang out in the background.

I stepped into the light of the pool house. I stood arm's length from the lifeless body of my dear sister. And then I saw it. The bloody knife. An antique silver knife from Grandma's set, passed down from four generations, now bloodied, discarded on the ground next to my dead sister's body.

My dead sister's body. My sister was dead. Is dead. Slashed to death in our very own home. It was all so horrible to imagine, I fell to my knees and vomited all over the hardwood floor, my refuse seeping into Ash's blood as Tabitha continued to wail.

Chapter Seven

I bent and set my bouquet down, adding it to the pile of roses already blocking the inscription on Ash's gravestone. A year after she was buried and someone still cared enough to bring her flowers. I didn't need to push aside the thorns to see the epitaph. Father had chosen a simple *Beloved Daughter*. It perfectly matched the stone just to the left, with the short descriptor *Beloved Mother*. I sensed a theme. If I passed into that dark night before my father, I'd be buried on the other side of Ash, no doubt spending eternity resting under my *Beloved Sister* stone. When Father joined us he'd be on the far left, the head of the Caulfield clan. I bet his epitaph was stipulated in his last will and testament or something. The tombstones were stark testimony to the truth of our family. We only existed in relation to Ash. I had never been my own person. I had always been my sister's sister. I wondered if that would change now that she was gone.

Looking at half my family resting side by side, and my own waiting grave, I couldn't help but wonder what was supposed to happen to Tabitha. Did Father plan to have her buried underneath him in the same plot? Or maybe she was just supposed to throw herself in on top of his casket like women were expected to do in India not too long ago?

Cemeteries had always brought out my morbid sense of

humor. That was one of the reasons I had chosen to come here alone, even though I knew I'd raised Father's ire by failing to join the official pilgrimage earlier in the day.

I could hardly believe that it had only been a year since Ash was murdered. Well, in some ways. In other ways it was hard to believe it had already been a year. Those first few weeks after her death went by in a blur while I walked around in a daze, barely even aware of the flurry of activities around me, as Tabitha made funeral arrangements, the police detectives traipsed in and out of the house, crime scene investigators swarmed around the pool house, and reporters skulked outside the gates of the estate like vultures waiting to pick over the remains of my family. With Mother and Ash gone, all there was left was not much more than bones.

The case made headlines that first month: pretty society girl killed on family estate, a string of casual acquaintances and even a couple of family friends were investigated, but there simply wasn't enough hard evidence to link anyone to the crime. We did learn a lot about our neighbors, including who was on the sex offender registry and whose kid had previous burglary convictions. Unfortunately, our neighbors learned equally disturbing things about us.

Both the local newspapers and the tabloids covered Ash's death, often with ridiculous claims like Father or I killed Ash or that Ash was still alive. *The Globe* went so far as to run an "Ash Sighting" column for three solid months.

I didn't know if the police ever took those leads seriously. I do know that Ash was the apple of Father's eye. I had never seen him raise a hand to her, no matter how much she thumbed her nose at him. I couldn't imagine he'd ever harm her. Plus, he and Tabitha were together, the maid was on the phone, and seemingly, I was the only one in the house without a solid alibi.

A few months later, Ash was in the ground and all the activity stopped. The house seemed deathly still in the absence of all that buzz. I had no idea what happened, where the detectives all went and why they seemed to lose interest in the case. I wondered if Father brought pressure to bear on them. Maybe the detectives were taking a hard look at our family and it made him nervous. Maybe he made a few calls to his cronies and suddenly the police were more interested in a different case, one that didn't involve a wealthy family. Maybe careful persuasion from the district attorney—a longtime family friend—kept the police from doing anything that would upset Father. A couple of the cops who were initially on the case left the department, and depending on which news account you believe, it was either over the intense criticism they had gotten in the press or over their conflicts with the higher-ups in actually attempting to solve Ash's murder.

Murder investigations of the rich or famous were often bungled because the cops were being careful not to offend and upset leading citizens. Maybe that was the case here. But could Father have been that selfish that he'd rather keep whatever dirty laundry he had secret than find the person who killed his beloved Daddy's girl? I don't know. No arrests had ever been made. The lead detective assured me the case was still open and would remain that way until they brought charges. But there was something about the way the guy said it—his eyes cast downward and his mustache twitching a bit—that told me he had little hope it would be solved.

I blamed Tabitha for that. I couldn't blame our loyal maid Maria, who compulsively cleaned up the scene before the police arrived. Or Father, who insisted on covering Ash with a sheet and wouldn't let the crime scene photographers do their job. But Tabitha knew better. She was enough of a *CSI* buff to know better than to go traipsing right through the scene, stepping in blood, pressing Ash against her chest, contaminating all the physical evidence. I hadn't helped the situation by adding my DNA to the pot. I didn't know they could get DNA from vomit.

But still, I blamed Tabitha. Because of her they'd probably never find my sister's killer. I feared he could be out there right now watching me. I could be next. I've heard enough crime shows to recognize that most murders are committed by someone close to the victim. But that wasn't who I imagined killed Ash. I pictured a strange man whose face was forever in the shadows and who, for some reason, would attack me next. It made me a little paranoid, always wondering if someone was following me, stalking me, waiting for the perfect moment to strike. I'd constantly look behind myself when walking, or stare in the rearview while driving, trying to determine if I was being followed.

It's hard to find a silver lining in a loved one's murder, even when that loved one was someone like Ash, who I hated to love and loved to hate. But if there *was* one good thing, it was that her death served as the impetus I needed to strike out on my own. And leaving home was the best decision I could have made— even if I didn't go far. In fact, I ended up moving into my sister's secret life. She apparently had bought an apartment, a clandestine apartment that must have been where she always disappeared to. I didn't even know she owned any property until that day, a few months after her death when her attorney placed the silver key in the palm of my hand.

The key was so cold against my skin, it provided no foreshadowing to what I would discover within the apartment's walls, no hint of the steamy double life Ash lived there. Why Ash had kept the place a secret, why she sent the key to her attorney directing him to pass it to me in the event of her death—those were just more mysteries to unfurl.

But before I could even begin to unravel those enigmas, I found my attention diverted by the other inheritance Ash left me: a box of her diaries.

Of course I started reading them. I had always wanted to get inside Ash's head, to understand who she was, and that impetus was all the stronger with her murder. After all, these private journals could provide a clue to uncovering her killer.

As much as I wanted to plow through them in a single sitting, I could only handle a page or two at a time because of the intensity of Ash's emotions—and the feelings they raised for me. It was sort of like she was still alive, just off in Europe or something, and she was writing me letters, finally wanting to get closer to me and divulging her secrets one by one. Sometimes her words would make me smile, and I could swear she was there in the room with me, watching me, laughing along with me.

There was a lot of seriousness too, a great deal of sadness—not just at the reminder of her absence, but about the things her diaries were revealing. But every page that I devoured put me one step closer to knowing my sister, my real sister, not the caricature she became in my eyes, especially over that last summer of her life.

I secretly hoped that these diaries wouldn't simply reveal who Ash was, but that they would expose her killer and help me uncover the truth about her death.

I flipped to a random page.

June 27

I know my sister looks down at me. That poor girl all alone in her room, reading her novels one after another, but watching me from the balcony. I don't know why she watches, why she's so repressed she just stares at me and every woman I bring home. Does she masturbate when she spies on us? Does she see us making love in the pool and fantasize about being with these women herself? I feel like a misfit in this family. My sister is prim and proper, every hair in its place, every word a calculated one. I wouldn't be surprised if she never had an orgasm. And Father, the uber-WASP, is even worse. Everything he does is controlled, designed to manipulate people into doing what he wants when he wants, and when he gets his way he doesn't care how you feel. I don't know how Tabitha puts up with it.

I don't care what my sister thinks of me, but it does

*hurt, the way she looks down her nose at me. I'm trash,
I know, pure trash out here, banished to the pool house
because I can't play by the rules, can't stay in school,
can't keep a job, can't keep my legs closed. I know I
can't keep on this way. Something's got to give in my
life. I know danger is out there, lurking in the shadows,
stalking me at every turn, but I don't know what to do
about it. I know I'm pushing it way too far. I just wish I
could have said no when it counted. But I can't, I never
can, never have.*

*I saw a woman today. A tall blonde with long hair
and green eyes who I had years ago at the Michigan
Womyn's Music Festival. Just a one-week-long fling of
sex and music and mud, where tofu seemed romantic
fare and moonlight and folk music was enough to get
me there. It seems so long ago. I don't remember her
name, though I can picture her pussy, perfectly pink
and puckered, quite well. I saw her, the woman from
Michigan, today and I thought about the woman I was
then. So filled with hope and brightness and a chance
to be someone or something other than what I have
become. But she knew me when I was something other
than what I am now. What I am now is a shell, lost to
frivolities like romance and moonlight and folk music.
I considered saying hello, but instead I watched her get
lost in the crowd. I've become an empty shell while all
the women I've fucked have been swallowed up in the
crowd, forever faceless and nameless.*

I was lucky to live alone. I had made a few friends through
work and they all had roommates, but they didn't come with a
trust fund, and none of them were left property by their dead

siblings. I didn't tell them about mine, but I was certain they had seen enough in the papers to deduce a thing or two about how I could afford to live where I did on my journalist's salary. Being alone worked for me. It was a relief.

While I hadn't become the person I swore I'd be after Shane—free of all emotional attachments—I had managed to avoid any serious relationships. In the year since, I had never once let someone in the way I did with Shane. But I hadn't been able to block her out entirely. I still thought of her often. Shane tried to talk to me after Ash's murder, first the day of the funeral, after we'd lowered her casket into the ground and tossed dirt in afterward. Even in the final days of summer it seemed such a cold and ignoble end. I decided right there that I wanted to be cremated when it was my time.

I was walking back to the limousine, trailing behind Father, who was half carrying, half dragging Tabitha, who was mute and ashen like a porcelain doll after she collapsed during the service, crumpling to the ground. Only Father's strong arms prevented her from falling right into the grave.

I was lost in my head, dreaming of what-ifs, when Shane stepped out from behind a tree, scaring me half to death.

"Megan," Shane said, her face drawn into a stern grimace. "We have to talk."

I just stared at her. It was like her words had been spoken in a foreign language I couldn't understand. I shook my head. I looked back at my feet and urged them to move. I stepped forward.

Shane moved in front of me, blocking my path. "Megan," she pleaded. "*Please.*"

I looked up again and caught her eyes. They burned into my own. I opened my mouth to speak, but before I could I heard my name being called again. This time it was Father's bellowing baritone and it pulled me back to reality and my desire to avoid speaking to Shane ever again. I tried to move on, but Shane grabbed my arm.

That was a mistake.

"Get your hands off my daughter!" Father roared. He had shuffled Tabitha into the limo and was thundering toward us.

"You'd better go," I hissed the warning.

She must have realized the danger she was in because she took off running.

Father missed tackling her by a few yards. "God damn paparazzi!" he spat.

I didn't correct his misassumption. If he'd realized who it was things would have been worse for Shane, and me. Father despised all of Ash's ex-lovers, but he seemed to hold a special hatred for the "biker dyke," speaking as though Shane was somehow more emblematic of Ash's Caligula-style descent into debauchery. Plus, he clearly thought Shane made an excellent suspect in her murder.

Although I knew better I harbored my own ill will toward the woman who broke my heart.

Shane approached me again and again at the bar until I finally stopped going to the E-room entirely.

By the time a year had passed, I was no longer too hostile to listen when Shane showed up once more. But I did figure anything Shane had to say was probably all bullshit anyway. Then again, maybe she just wanted to soothe her guilty conscience and who was I to prevent her from apologizing to me? It was the kind of thing I secretly longed for—that all those who'd done me wrong in the past would be driven by remorse to seek me out and express their deepest regret. It could happen. Couldn't it? "I spent all those days at the pool trying to get a chance to talk to you," Shane insisted the last time we spoke. Oh please, that's on par with "she fell on my dick" as an excuse for infidelity. I wanted to hear her admit her wrongdoing and take responsibility for the pain she'd caused me.

And I wanted to confront her again about the engine I'd heard the night Ash died, the engine I'd never told the police about because I'd always secretly feared it had been Shane's motorcycle, and I didn't want to be the one placing her at the scene of Ash's murder. During my previous attempt to get the truth, Shane had been adamant that she was nowhere near the estate that night, that she was at home alone, with no one around to corroborate her story. I didn't believe her. I thought she just wasn't ready to be honest with herself or me. I hadn't seen her since.

I had moved on. I moved into Portland, and now my days were filled with work at the *Willamette Week*, a local alternative newspaper.

Then one night I finally relented and went out with a group of friends, celebrating my recent promotion from flunky to editorial assistant. We were drinking microbrews at a lesbian bar called the Mint, laughing and passing gossip around the table like salt, and up walks Shane, cool as Ocean's Eleven, asking if anyone would mind her joining our group. What balls! I had forgotten the impact the mere sight of Shane had on me, on my body. I hated her, but just having her in proximity to me was like a magnet pulling me to her, a palsy forcing my knees apart, a flood soaking my panties.

Just like the conniving bastards they were, my friends conspired to leave me alone with Shane. To their credit, they didn't know the whole story and had only seen the way my eyes lit up when she sauntered over. They also knew it had been quite a while since anyone had brushed the cobwebs from my undercarriage, and being good friends, wanted to arrange my servicing. So one by one, they slipped away until by the end of the night, I was left drinking alone with Shane.

I couldn't deny the chemical attraction I'd once had to her. And though I'd managed to keep it in check for a year, it all came flooding back, right there in the fucking bar. It was enticing.

Damn it. I couldn't say no to her.

We ended up back at my place, at Ash's place, and I shoved her onto the bed. Which should tell you that this wasn't anything like the sex we had before. There was no sweet tenderness, no head to toe kissing. It was fast and raw and I was in control of the entire encounter. I fucked her good. I was more in control than even Shane realized. I had learned a thing or two from living in my sister's love shack. Unbeknownst to Shane, I was taping the entire encounter. And when I was finished, chagrined at myself for not saying "No" to begin with, I rolled over and demanded that she let herself out—as soon as possible.

April 18

I love power. I don't think there's anything wrong with admitting that, is there? I'm turned on by power. I am Father's daughter in that way. Life is all about power. Sex is all about power. Life is all about sex. Life is all the sweeter with power. These are the things that give me power:

1. *riding on the back of a motorcycle*
2. *controlling pain, usually mine*
3. *making videos of people in compromising positions*
4. *bagging wealthy babes*
5. *banging doctor's wives*
6. *emotional control*
7. *dumping people who still want me*
8. *fucking the daughters of Daddy's clients*
9. *then telling him all about it*
10. *fucking Daddy's and Tabitha's best friends. Both of them. Together.*

That was a fun night. Milly and John Castleford were two stuck up WASPs until you got them in the sack and then they turned into She-beast and the Fuckinator. John liked to be sucked, and you know a good girl like Milly wouldn't do that, so I did it and then took it up the ass while Milly came in my mouth again and again. I think it may have been Milly's first orgasm. It worked for me too, because even though I was only eighteen, I just kept thinking repeatedly how angry Daddy and Tabitha would be if they saw me ass up with the brandy and croquet set, much less their best friends. And Milly and John came back for more and more, eventually getting kinkier and kinkier with me until at some point I had to cut them off because I got bored.

That's the beauty of power too. You have more of it when you don't flaunt it. You hold on to it, knowing full well that one day you'll put it to good use. Do I tell everyone what I'm doing at the time? No. Coach Harting doesn't need to know that I'm schtupping his wife Peggy. I'll give her a little pickle tickle and leave her wanting for more, and when I need something, well, I'll call Peggy or Father and remind them just how Coach would feel about all this.

I get bored a lot, but I've discovered a new source of power. It comes in a little package, but it packs a big wallop, like the best ones always do. It's given me a new game to play. Let's call it Sex, Lies and Videotape. *It's amazing how tiny those cameras are these days. My little secret was a package deal, a couple of cameras (multiple angles being all the rage), and recording equipment that gets triggered by a motion detector. Technofucking fabulous.*

I even got my own little secret fuck hut prepared for my new little gizmo. I had some overly curious handyman wall off half of the walk-in closet, making a nice little fuck hut where the cameras roll all night long. He did such a good job even I can't tell where the old wall ends and new work begins, and since the guy was used to creating panic rooms for his ritzier clientele, he made it so the passage in and out disappeared into the wall and the cameras are completely undetectable. I get kind of horny just thinking about it. I rigged the rest of the room myself. No need having mister working class curiosity finger my love swing and other toys when the contraptions were so easy to hook up.

Did I think twice about taping other people? All those women traipsing in and out of my panties? I know there are repercussions to power, there would be for me if I were to reveal who and what I was doing even now. But I won't tell and neither will she. Or will she?

Ash was filming herself? I thought as soon as I read those final paragraphs. Having sex? Oh, my God, was it still on? Had it been turning on every time I came in to my bedroom? I started to panic. What if it was being broadcast to someone else?

Holy fuck, what if it had a live feed to a Web site? I was suddenly filled with paranoia and dread. I had to find that camera right that very instant. I dropped the journal unceremoniously and darted into the bedroom. I ripped down wall coverings, ran my fingers along every inch of the sheetrock, trying to sense the seam in the plaster. Nothing.

I moved into the closet, yanking outfits, hanger and all, off the rod and tossing them in a pile on the floor. I picked up shoes by the armful and flung them toward the bed. Finally, I had space to walk to the far end of closet and feel around in the dark until I found what I was looking for. Who puts a cable TV outlet in a closet? I fiddled with the metal plug and eventually the wall gave way under my hand, a panel moved to the side. A slight turn to the side and I meandered through.

I couldn't believe my eyes. This wasn't just a camera room, a secret private vanity space that Ash could hide away in, taping people on both sides of the doors, and scurrilously watching the DVDs later. No, this was her own shrine to Eros, a room of pleasure, and by the looks of it, pain. Upon whom was it inflicted, though? Along one side of the room was a shelf with a large screen TV atop a black shelving unit. On each shelf sat a stack of baskets with labels on each that read like they were straight out of a porn movie: "gags," "plugs," "nipple fun," "floggers," "vibes," "strap-ons," "electro." I wasn't even sure what a couple of them could possibly hold, but I was too flushed taking it all in to even go dig through the baskets. Standing there felt like walking into the Hustler Store and discovering that my sister lived in the place. There wasn't a bed, but where you'd expect one sat this gloriously delicious lipstick red suede playpen sectional sofa, which took up nearly half of the diminutive room. It was squared off on all sides so you sat on the sofa and slowly slid down into a bed-like flat area that was penned in on all sides. Lying on the sofa felt like a cross between being in a child's playpen and an orgy den, and the sheer surprise of that dichotomy was so alarming that I wanted to rush out and forget all about Ash's fuck den. But I didn't because, as much as I was appalled, I was equally drawn to this room and to what it represented, and to Ash's role as some sort of sexual provocateur. When I came back to my senses, I remembered my initial reason for breaking through that veiled partition: to find Ash's videos. I started sifting through the containers on the cabinet, trying to focus less on the instruments of pleasure—or torture—that made up the contents and look only for the sexy surveillance videos Ash had mentioned in her diary. Not surprisingly, the large black rectangular box jutting out from the bottom shelf and labeled "Punani" contained dozens of DVDs, meticulously labeled with a code I wasn't sure I wanted to crack.

CHAPTER EIGHT

M egan, there's a Shane on line two."
Who gave her my work number? Probably one of my damn nosy friends. Great. Who knew how I'd be able to dodge her now.

"Hello, Shane. What can I do for you?"

"Well, that's formal. Okay then, can I see you again?"

"No, sorry, not going to happen."

I didn't want to see her again. I got everything I needed the other night. That was a display of weakness on my part. I had vowed not to let anyone in, much less Shane, and there I was, taking her calls again.

I didn't care that Father suspected Shane was involved in Ash's murder and insisted I stay away from her because she supposedly had a criminal record, which probably meant she was busted drinking underage. I didn't care that she was home alone all night when Ash was killed—an alibi that was beyond flimsy—or that the cops had hauled her in for questioning.

I knew Shane and she might have been a terrible girlfriend, but she was no killer. Plus, she was as enthralled with my sister as any of them. Why on earth would she kill her? Still, our last encounter was a mistake, a one-time need on my part that shouldn't erase the way she treated me, fucking my sister and then flaunting it by the pool for weeks after. I didn't want to be with her, not the way I did that summer so long ago when I was a love-struck little baby dyke. Maybe I wasn't as jaded as Ash was but I was starting to understand a bit of what drove her, and I could see that there was a little part of that inside of me. Apparently last night, that little part reigned supreme, but that didn't mean I'd give in to my base urges again.

Shane called again. And again. And again. In fact, Shane called twice a day, every day for the next week. Finally, I listened to her explain, "It wasn't by accident I ran into you at the Mint. I tracked you down."

I hung up. Undaunted, Shane showed up at my office the next day. And the day after that. Finally, on the third day, more out of embarrassment than anything else, I relented and agreed to cocktails at Saucebox, a trendy nightclub eatery where the noise was such a roar it kept all conversations quick.

What I hadn't planned was how much I would need to lean toward her in order to hear even half the words Shane was saying. By the time the two cocktails in front of us had a few empties in their wake, I was practically sitting in her lap. Shane had her lips pressed to my ear, telling me about her job as the editor of a women's poetry journal. I didn't realize she worked in publishing. I didn't know much about Shane at all. For example, I would never have guessed that just the slightest tickle of her breath on the ridge of my ear would send chills down my spine.

After a few more Washington Red Appletinis and some supplementary ear play, I started to forget just what I hated so much about Shane. I started to forget about her betrayal. I started to forget about my dead sister. I started to forget about everything, except how much I wanted Shane, how much I'd always wanted her. There was nothing left but the noise of the club and my passion for this woman.

I took her home again, only this time I didn't film our encounter. I still kicked her out of bed, but not until I woke up in the morning, the sound of mouse feet blasting holes in my head. When I rolled over and found Shane next to me all smiles, I threw up. I don't know if it was her, the alcohol, or the alien that burrowed into my stomach and died. I allowed her to clean herself—and me—before sending her away, calling in sick and, like any good addict, swearing I'd give up my vices for good if only God would mute the world for one day.

It wasn't my fault he didn't keep his end of the bargain.

When I crawled out of my alcohol-induced coma I realized that I still had yet to hear Shane utter those three magic words, and until she did I absolutely, positively could not spend another minute with her.

I ignored her calls for a few days and then finally instructed our receptionist to give Shane the message—I wouldn't take her calls until I was assured I would hear that expression: *I am sorry.*

The flowers arrived within the hour. There were three giant bouquets in all, one of red roses, another of yellow roses, and one of purple hyacinths. A balloon drifted above the hyacinths. I turned it around and saw the words printed there: "I'm sorry."

Overwhelmed by emotion, my hands were shaking so badly that I couldn't pull the small card from its envelope. Our receptionist took it from me and read aloud, "The hyacinths are an apology, the yellow roses an offer of friendship, and the red roses to tell you that my feelings for you have never changed."

She ended to a chorus of "aw" and a round of clapping as my coworkers took it upon themselves to intrude in my personal business. Swayed by the scent of forgiveness exuding from the group of women who huddled so tightly around me I felt like slapping asses and throwing a pigskin, I took Shane's call and agreed to meet with her one more time. However, this time I insisted on staying as far away from the intoxicating allure of alcohol and suggested coffee at Haven.

She was there when I arrived, chatting amiably with the barista, but when she saw me outside she rushed over and held the door like a gentleman. I waved her aside, made my order, and joined her at a table in the corner.

I fought the knee-jerk impulse to thank her for the flowers. "You have ten minutes," I said, hoping I sounded brusque, flippant even.

"Thank you for meeting with me, Megan. I know it's been tough on you."

"Hmm." I took another drink from my mocha.

"Okay, okay. I'll get right to the point. I don't want to speak ill of the dead—"

But I'm going to anyway, I imagined her saying. Why did people always use that phrase to preface doing exactly that? If they didn't want to speak ill of the dead, why did they speak up at all? Shane wasn't winning any points from me.

"But you know how manipulative your sister was. She always seemed able to manipulate me into doing things, even when it was some elaborate joke at my expense. Which is what happened that night you, uh, it's what happened that night."

You mean the night I walked in on you fucking my sister? I wanted to scream it so everyone in the café, everyone in the neighborhood, hell, everyone in the whole damn town could bear witness to the awful thing Shane had done to me. But I didn't shout it out. I didn't even mutter it. I just rolled my eyes and shook my head.

Shane barreled on, although she at least had the decorum to lower her voice. "I swear, I didn't go there intending to have sex with her." Her eyes pleaded with me to believe her and I wasn't sure if it was my heart or my cunt, but some part of me really wanted to.

"I went to see you, but you weren't back from the awards ceremony. Ash said I could wait for you in the pool house and offered me a drink." Shane swallowed hard. She tried to hold my gaze, but I looked away.

"The next thing I know," Shane continued, "you're opening the door and I'm wondering how the hell I got there."

I snorted. "So what? You blacked out? She drugged you? What are you saying?"

It was Shane's turn to shake her head. "I don't know. I've gone over that night again and again, and it just doesn't make sense. I mean, it wasn't like she forced me, but it sort of felt like I wasn't a willing participant. And then afterward it was so clear that she'd planned the entire thing."

"Oh, right. Why would she do that?"

"To hurt you."

I stared at her. "Wait. What? You're saying Ash forced you to have a threesome with her just to hurt me? That doesn't even make sense. Why?" I was at loss for words. I just shook my head again, pushed my chair back, and started to stand up.

Shane's hand on my arm stopped me. Even through my blouse her touch sent electric shivers radiating out from where her fingers landed. "For all her faults, Megan, your sister loved you very much, even if she didn't know how to show it. She and I had some history. I wasn't that great to her." Shane pursed her lips and glanced down at her lap. "She just didn't want you to get hurt."

"But by your logic, she set that night up to deliberately hurt me!"

"No. I mean, yes, she did. But she was trying to save you more pain later on if you fell in love with me and I broke your heart. Only Ash didn't realize I'd never…" Shane trailed off. "Look, it's not like I'm asking you to forgive me straight off. I did something terrible. You know firsthand the kind of charismatic power Ash had over people. I hoped that you might give me a second chance because of that."

I couldn't do it.

Not that night, at any rate. A few days later I let her give it the good ol' college try. Everyone deserves a second chance. And a second orgasm. Shane gave them in spades. And my sexual needs were starting to be more pressing than my emotional ones. That night I didn't kick her out of bed when we were done.

The next morning we were in the kitchen making omelets—whore's breakfast, Ash used to call it—like a giddy couple, and I wondered if I could ever let myself have feelings for Shane again.

The omelets led back to bed, which led to dinner, which led to more sex, and before I knew it, one weekend together turned into a full-fledged affair. After a few months of coupledom, things seemed idyllic, almost normal even. I loved the safety of it, the maturity of it, and without even realizing it, I'd let my guard down again, allowing myself to feel the emotions I'd always harbored for Shane.

❖

"What's going on, baby?" It was my turn to query Shane. I doubted that I came across as threatening as I felt, but I was certain my tone had a hostile edge to it. Shane had stood me up for dinner half a dozen times now, and whenever we were together she seemed distant. We had been dating six months, and already the honeymoon was over.

"Nothing." Shane was sullen, uncommunicative.

"God damn it, Shane. Would you just fucking talk to me?" I was so sick of her silent treatment I felt like shoving a fork in my thigh just to get a reaction from her. Maybe I was more angry at myself than Shane. I'd given in, I allowed her to suck me into her world again and now she was going cold—again. I should've been strong, should've stayed committed to the plan.

I still wanted to solve Ash's murder, still felt Shane's recollections from that evening might be the break I needed, but Shane didn't want to talk about Ash, and I didn't want to keep fighting, so I shelved it all, putting my life on the back burner to make someone else happy. *Again.*

I hated myself for the ways in which I changed around a woman I loved. Or at least this woman, being as she had been the only woman I had loved, I didn't have a lot to compare it to. But with Shane, I felt like I lost control somehow, like I forgot who I was. Who was that? Maybe I'd never known who I was. Or maybe I knew and I just didn't like it.

I was trying so hard to be strong and independent. I wanted to be successful on my own terms, you know, not to feel like everything I had and everything I was sprouted from Father's money. Wasn't my begging for an iota of attention from Shane similar to Father controlling me with his purse strings? Well, fuck her.

"Look, Shane, if you don't want to be in this relationship, then fine by me. You started it." I was walking to the door of the apartment, ready to throw her shit out, when she turned around and looked at me like she was seeing me for the first time, and it kind of surprised her.

"I do want to be here, Megan. It's just that things have gotten a little dull." God, the mind games this girl played!

"Dull? Dull? What the hell, Shane? It's been six months and you're already bored?" I couldn't believe she'd tired of me already. It seemed like she had spent longer wooing me than she had bedding me. *What the fuck?* I couldn't believe I fell for her shit again.

"No, it's not that. I just think we should shake things up."

I didn't reply. There was nothing I wanted to say to her. Hadn't I just settled down for her, because of her? Wasn't this what she wanted? I couldn't believe Shane had the audacity to complain about our domesticity.

In truth, I was terrified she was right, like I'd tricked her into thinking I was exciting, that I was just a younger version of Ash, not the dull person whose inexperience in bed made her lovemaking so tedious that her lover couldn't bear the monotony.

What did that mean anyway? Was this code for threesomes? Polyamory? Or did it just mean Shane wanted to pull out a copy of the *Kama Sutra* and try out some new positions? I wouldn't admit it, but I feared that if I refused to even consider enlivening our relationship, it would give Shane reason to leave me and worse, it would reveal how much of a sexual dullard I really was.

Maybe all couples eventually reached a point in their relationship where they needed to shake things up. Maybe it just went by so fast because Shane's so experienced. Maybe other lesbians knew how to keep their lovers more entertained. God.

I bet Ash never had this problem, never had someone imply she had become boring in bed. No, everything I'd learned about Ash told me she was the one wanting to shake things up. Thinking of Ash, I could almost see her laughing at me for being so insipid and naïve.

Well, I wasn't going to let Shane slip through my fingers after all we'd been through. And I refused to allow my fear to paralyze me. If Shane wanted spice, I was determined to give her habañero peppers. I'd show her. I'd shake things up. Tonight I was going to start watching Ash's sex DVDs.

I could kill two birds with one stone. I could help find out what happened to Ash and maybe discover what magic spell my sister cast over every woman that she met. Surely I could find some pointers to impress Shane in the bedroom. Delving into Ash's secrets and keeping Shane intrigued seemed reason enough to watch what could be some sordid recordings.

Yet, even as I was putting the DVD in the player, I couldn't help but wonder how smart it was to watch my sister getting it on. I mean, the summer she died I had seen her having sex many times, but always from a distance. This would be close-up and personal images of my deceased sibling. That could very well cross some invisible line separating decent folks from the perverse. What if this video was like Pandora's box and would unleash something I could never put back?

Although I was quite serious, I imagined that Japanese horror film where a scary zombie girl would come slithering out of the television after viewers watched a particular videotape. Then they'd die of fright. I couldn't believe enough time had passed that I could have such a morbid thought and laugh, not cry, that my big sister was dead and I was sitting in her old apartment watching videos of her fucking other people.

Ash moved into the frame, naked except for a scarf around her neck and white go-go boots that came up to her knees. Two women entered the room, one of them large, foreboding, and the other rather diminutive. Both women were fully clothed in black leather and denim. They each had dog collars around their necks and giant dildos popping out of their jeans. The large woman, a blonde with multiple tattoos and a black dildo, had a chain that stretched from her cock ring to a back pocket. She went behind Ash, weaving her arms through Ash's and pulling her backward so she was splayed across a console table. The smaller woman, this one dark-haired, maybe Mediterranean, shoved Ash's legs apart, then pushed one of Ash's legs up in the air and the other to the side, posing her like a porn model, all the while navigating a pink dildo into Ash. Ash winced, then smiled at the camera. It was her camera, after all. Did the other women even know they were being filmed? Maybe not.

But Ash certainly did, and even though there was no sound on it, I could tell she was calling the shots in the scene because her lips moved before anything new happened. I found that comforting. I didn't have to worry about consent when Ash was clearly commanding them, directing them with what to do and when. Ash had asked to be splayed over this table, taken by two butches with piercings and giant cocks.

And take her they did, moving in and out of her for what seemed like hours. Ash smiled at the camera and whispered again to her lovers. It was creepy to see her looking right at me, so I hit the fast-forward button and the blonde jumped into action, shoving her cock inside Ash's mouth.

In high speed, Ash yanked the scarf from around her neck and wrapped the ends around her wrists, jammed her hands inside the blonde's, and tugged. I slowed down, trying to understand what she was trying to say. It seemed like she wanted to be choked.

The blonde shook her head, refusing, but Ash was demanding, so she gently, very gingerly tugged at the scarf. Ash berated her. I recognized the look. Her partner relented, tightening the scarf. Ash smiled at the camera again and then threw her head back in ecstasy. The camera faded out.

I rummaged around through the closet, tossing aside my own clothes to sift through the things Ash left behind. I had something specific in mind. A little while later, I opened the bedroom door and came out wearing nothing but white go-go boots and a long scarf. Rather than widening in delight, Shane's eyes appeared saucerlike, as though she had seen a ghost. That wasn't the look I wanted to see on my lover's face. Had she seen my sister wear this outfit? Or was it just the sight of me in such an unexpected outfit that made her go pale? Did I turn her on? Or did I repel her?

Unwilling to be dissuaded, I decided to find out one way or the other. Trying not to show my embarrassment at showing my bare ass, I sauntered over to the couch and stood in front of her. Shane reached out with both hands, clearly intent on grabbing my butt cheeks and pulling me toward her. But tonight I was determined to be the one in control. I grabbed her left hand and raised it to my lips, parting them seductively as her fingers approached my mouth. Her whole body shifted forward, just as I had intended it to.

Rather than penetrating my mouth with her fingers, I stepped back, and used the momentum to yank her off the edge of the sofa. She stumbled forward and I turned around, leading her into the bedroom. Shane tried to push me onto the bed, but I shook my head and waved a schoolmarm finger at her for being such a naughty child. I tugged her down to her knees, flung one leg up against the dresser, and shoved her face between my thighs, pulling her hair a bit in order to keep myself steady. She ate it up, literally lapping me up like a dying man drinking straight from the spring in a desert oasis. She was mine all right, and I was going to show her why she was here.

Before I let myself reward her with an orgasm, I pulled her to her feet and shoved her onto the bed, before opening the armoire's top drawer, retrieving a package, and tossing it at her.

"What's this?" Shane asked.

I put my finger to my lips to shush her. *Patience, my pet*, I thought, watching her tear open the package. The corner of her top lip curled into a smug grin. I could see she was pleased with the new dildo I bought her, because she quickly strapped it on and it stood at attention with a stiffness Mark had never once been able to demonstrate.

I didn't speak, but mimed to her, allowing my mouth to slack open and pressing my flat hand over the O to indicate surprise at her very large blue and white marbled member that was clearly so happy to see me.

Playing along, Shane kept quiet, or to put it more accurately, she did not talk, although she was soon making quite a racket. As was I.

I pushed her onto her back and climbed aboard like a harlot who wanted her (wo)man-meat and nothing else. I drew the long scarf from my neck and instead of using it on myself, as Ash had done in the video, I used it on Shane.

But I had no experience with bondage or erotic asphyxiation, and I hadn't been a Boy Scout. Nor had I paid much attention to the knots on the riggings the few times I'd been out on friends' sailboats. Not knowing the difference between a noose and any other binding, and not ready to risk my lover's life for one night of pleasure, I decided to start slow. I tied Shane's wrists to the bedposts. She was compliant and tested the bindings to demonstrate their effectiveness in restricting her movement.

I rode her hard, watching her wince and moan and strain against the scarf that prevented her from grabbing me by the hips and positioning me where she wanted. Instead, I shifted my weight around, judging from the look on her face and my own pleasure to determine the best angles.

I was riding her and slamming my pelvis up and down around

the shaft of her cock, and all at once I pictured whipping her with a riding crop and imagined her riding me this way with spurs. The notion brought me right to that point where I was about to blow, and I could see from Shane's face that she was just as ready as I, and right before I let go, I turned and smiled at the camera.

June 1

I'm worried about kiddo. I think Megan wants to be like me, to emulate me and my life. But it's a life of such dreadful emptiness and need I wouldn't wish it on anyone, especially my beautiful sister. I feel like I have a huge hole in the middle of my soul that I've been trying to fill with an endless parade of lovers: women, men, going back to, hell, how long has it been? I don't know, since I was a teenager, for sure, since the big one, the first one, the only one that really mattered. Sometimes I'm numb. No, usually I'm numb. Sometimes I want to feel pain, just so I can feel something. Choke me, fuck me, hit me, burn me; but do it with a hint of tenderness. I want to feel something besides empty pain. A punishment with kisses.

I've slept with over a hundred women at this point, especially if you count all the Dinah Shore festivals and Michigan madness and the play parties and that one weekend. Oh, that weekend. But all those notches on my lipstick case aside, I still feel empty. With all the sexual exploration I've engaged in during my twenty-six years, my life still feels so devoid of intimacy it's a fucking joke. It's so crazy that I still believe in love, still want to be with The One. But will I ever? I envy Megan for her innocence, her naiveté. I hope she never becomes who I have become. I hope she never has to go through what I've been through. I hope she never sees the world for what it is, the stinking cesspool of filth and betrayal.

Chapter Nine

There was a new girl at the office, a reporter named Paula, with hair so curly it seemed like it had been transplanted from another part of her body. *Hello, Hair Club for Men.* She called it a jewfro, though she was Irish, so I was not really sure if it was okay to repeat her colorful language. Was it racist?

I nicknamed her Curly Q because she was bubbly and quirky with perfect little features—the upturned nose, the sparkling violet eyes, the puckered lips, and perpetually rosy cheeks. Paula seemed like she liked me. She'd been hanging around my cubicle every day at work, bringing me Twizzlers and mocha and asking me out to lunch or drinks. I assumed she was hitting on me, and I was enjoying it, playing various kinky scenarios in my mind like a series of short porno trailers for a best of compilation, until we went out to dinner and I discovered her true motive.

"I know about Shane and Ashley," Paula revealed almost innocently. I was immediately appalled to hear anyone mention their names together. I was particularly perturbed that a colleague from work would bring them up.

"I'm sorry, what?" I honestly didn't know where this was going.

"Look, I'll be honest with you, Megan. I have an ulterior motive in befriending you," Paula confessed. "I want to write a book about your sister's murder and I'd like your cooperation."

Apparently Paula had true crime aspirations from her time on the police beat at the *Oregonian*, and when she discovered she could be working alongside me at the *Willamette Week*, she was determined to use that connection to write and sell her own based on real life *In Cold Blood*–style thriller. Paula said she'd already had interest from a publisher, particularly regarding the love triangle angle.

"Love triangle?" I could feel my cheeks burn. Ash. Cynthia. Shane. I couldn't help but picture their naked bodies entwined. I tried to push the image away, replacing it with Shane holding me, explaining what happened that day. I told myself eyewitnesses were unreliable, even when they were me.

"I know you and your sister were fighting over your girlfriend, Shane—"

"So you think I killed her? My own sister? Jesus." I shook my head until my teeth rattled. How could anyone think I was capable of murder?

"I didn't say that," Paula protested. "I just think it's an intriguing element to the story. You don't think your love triangle played a part in her death."

It wasn't a question, but I answered as though it was. "Look, Paula, I don't know what the fuck you think you know, but you've got it all wrong." In the eighteen months since Ash's death I'd become familiar with many of the local reporters, their style and techniques, and I had developed a way of dealing with them all. But Paula's insinuations—her straightforward accusations— threw me. "Get this straight, I did not kill my sister!"

"Hey, Megan, I'm on your side, I'm not saying—"

"Bullshit you're on my side. I can't believe the preposterousness of you taking me to dinner to do research for your book. And then you accuse me of being the cause of Ash's death."

"You mean murder."

"Her murder," I repeated. "Neither I nor Shane had anything to do with her *murder*. And if you knew anything you'd realize that Ash would never fight with me, or anyone else, over one of her many conquests."

"You're right," she said in what I thought was an apology. "I understand your sister *was* quite the slut."

"You bitch!" I shoved the table away and flung the remains of my blended mocktail on Paula's smug little perfect face.

She smiled. "Of course," she said, dabbing the drink from her brow with a napkin, "I can't imagine it was your sister who was the jealous one." Paula smirked.

Wow, this bitch is unflappable. Meanwhile, I was shaking and my voice started cracking when I shot back, "I'm getting a restraining order in the morning." Like that was going to happen, and then I burst out crying and couldn't get out of there fast enough.

I ran from the restaurant and tumbled into a cab where I sobbed all the way back to the apartment. I was still bawling when I got there, hoping that Shane would do her part to soothe me. Instead, there was a note on the fridge: "We're in production, had to go back to the office. See you tomorrow. Love, Shane."

Fuck, fuck, fuck. Fuck it all to hell. I had a dead sister, a cold girlfriend, a calculating reporter, and a father so rigid he wouldn't know empathy if it bit him on the ass. I couldn't believe all of this was happening to me. I mean, I recognized that I was the sister who lived, but I still couldn't bear feeling like no matter what I did, I couldn't fucking win. Sometimes I wished I were the one who was dead. The dead had it easy.

The next morning I had to be at the paper before our family attorney's office was open, so I hoped I could just avoid Paula until I talked with him about the possibility of getting a restraining order based on nothing but a few rude comments and her blaming me for my sister's murder. Maybe this could be one of those times where Father's money and standing in the community would grease the wheels of justice and shake loose the paperwork I wanted.

In the meantime, surely I could at least tell my boss, right? But Paula was an experienced reporter and I was just an editorial assistant, so who would a publisher keep? Probably her. I just read submissions, answered complaint letters, and wrote calendar copy. You didn't need talent or a degree to do that. But Paula had bylines. Plus, she wasn't the one refusing to work within five hundred feet of another employee. Still. I was here first.

Before I could march into the publisher's office, my cell phone rang with a call from a girl I was fairly collegial with at *Just Out*, the local gay newspaper.

"Have you seen the blogs?"

"No," I honestly replied. "What's up?"

She inhaled sharply, as though deciding how much to tell me. I was nervous as hell. "Just tell me! What's going on?" The pregnant pause was freaking me out.

"All right. Someone posted something on SheWired.com alleging that you've been in a long-term relationship with the number one suspect in your sister's murder!"

That bitch, Paula.

"A bunch of local bloggers picked it up and are reprinting it. And so did Perez Hilton."

"Wait, what? *Who?*"

"They're all anonymous posts, but the blogosphere seems pretty captivated by it. Even our bloggers are posting the gossip and, well, I heard the police were paying attention too. I just thought you should know."

Oh, my God, how was this even possible? Obviously, this was Paula's doing. But how could she just have made something up and then posted it anonymously and instantly get it accepted as fact? God, it was so fucking unfair.

"Wait, why would Perez Hilton reprint it? It's not like we're celebrities."

"Oh, well, uh," my tipster stammered, clearly uncomfortable

blurting out the problem. "Well, you should read his, um, it's, I think you should read it. Look, Megan, I gotta go. I just wanted to warn you, okay? Hang in there."

With that, she was gone. I snapped my cell phone closed and ducked into the nearest Starbucks—in Portland never more than a few feet away—where I was lucky enough to find an empty terminal and log on to Perezhilton.com. As soon as it loaded I wanted to put my hands over the screen to hide the page from the other patrons. It wasn't a PG image. At first I thought I'd stumbled onto a pop-up ad for a porn site. Then I looked closer. I recognized the star on the XXX video still. We happened to have DNA in common.

The story was there too, right on the front page, above the digital fold.

> Well, well, we have news from the naughty today as insiders tell me that Ashley Caulfield, aka porn star Pookie Michaels, was involved in a lesbian love triangle with her own sister! The younger sister, Megan Caulfield, is a reporter at the *Willamette Week* in Portland, Oregon. Meanwhile, the third leg in this sordid triangle, Shane Ryan, a female editor at the *Women's Poetry Journal*, is Caulfield's on-and-off-again lover (currently on). Michaels, who came to fame (pun intended) in the amateur film *Muff Diving Miss Daisy*, was stabbed to death last July. No one has officially been named in connection with her murder, though Ryan is apparently considered a suspect. No word yet on the Sapphic sister's involvement in the homicide, but talk about sibling rivalry! Crazy lesbionics!

I couldn't help but read it over and over again. Then I Googled my name and discovered links to at least a dozen other blogs. Gossip spreads like wildfire on the Web. I wasn't sure what was worse: being implicitly named a suspect, being romantically linked to an overt suspect, or discovering my sister was an amateur porn star. God, I hope she was an amateur. This would totally kill Father if he found out. I'd never thought about whether Father was a porn aficionado or not. I mean, I assumed he watched porn, even if I couldn't imagine where or when. He must've, though, right? Didn't all men? Still, it was disturbing to think about Father stumbling onto scenes starring Ash. But that's exactly what I had done. And having stumbled onto my sister's homemade sex videos, I didn't destroy them, didn't take a hammer to the DVDs and reduce them to shards. No, I deliberately watched them. And then I acted them out. I felt like vomiting again.

Clearly, Paula had been one busy beaver last night, planting gossip on blogs to stir the pot and lend credence to her own theory of the crime—that Shane or I killed Ash. In doing so Paula might have given my lawyer more to work with, but how could I counter her allegations? They were preposterous, but everyday folks wouldn't understand that. At best, they'd think I was the slut banging my dead sister's girlfriend, when it had been the other way around, and at worst, they'd think I was the killer myself.

It was all too much to handle, and though I couldn't wait to ream Paula, I couldn't bear to walk into the *Willamette Week* offices this morning. I called my editor from the coffee shop and feigned sick. I was pretty certain he knew what was going on, but he sounded sympathetic and told me to "take care of myself now" almost as though I'd never be coming back.

Was he right? Was this it for my career? Just because I didn't need the job—financially—didn't mean I wanted to lose it. Plus, I needed it for my résumé, right? Who's going to hire me with a blank sheet of paper? Or worse, once they learn I was fired from the only position listed because everyone thought I was a homicidal slut? A friend of Father's? I shuddered at the thought.

CHAPTER TEN

By the time Father phoned, inviting me to the house for dinner over the weekend, I had already called in sick twice and avoided Shane a full week. I spent the rest of my time reading Ash's journals and viewing her sex videos. The latest was probably the most shocking to date, and featured a scene I couldn't quite shake.

In it, Ash was wearing a black flapper dress with pearls and what I could only describe as Victorian hooker boots, even though such a thing probably never existed. A black mask completely covered her eyes. A tall, thin, and beautiful woman I'd never seen before held Ash's hand and led her into a room with a mattress on the floor in between four metal posts that looked like modern horseshoe crooks. There were candles everywhere, from the floors to the windowsills.

Inside the room, there were a bunch of other women all partially naked and wearing macabre black and white masks that looked like bird beaks on a yin yang symbol. Some women had gold chains around their waists that linked to rings in their noses or ran down and disappeared in their crotches. Others had pink leather paddles or cat-o'-nine-tails with handles woven in white and pink buckskin. Still others wore ridiculously large dildos, giant ebony cocks larger than anything I'd ever seen in real life. The production values on the film were far inferior, but otherwise the video struck me as a cross between *Eyes Wide Shut* and *Lair of the White Worm.*

Except there were so many women. Every configuration of woman seemed to have joined Ash in that room: young, old, fat, thin, black, white, brown, yellow, butch, femme. Although some looked vaguely familiar, the masks successfully obscured their faces. I only knew Shane's body well enough to identify in a naked lineup, and thankfully, she wasn't among the women in the room.

A pair of fuzzy pink handcuffs strapped Ash's wrists to one set of posts and her knees inched up to her chest before two women pulled her legs, forcing them down and using another pair of fuzzy cuffs to strap her ankles down at the end of the bed.

Within moments each woman was taking turns doing rather unspeakable things to Ash, their meaty paws tearing the straps off her dress, pulling the top down to expose her breasts while pushing the rest up above her waist. She was wearing a gold chain around her waist too but no panties. Was this an initiation? It looked almost like a ritual, but I couldn't tell how much of it was fantasy orchestrated by Ashley and how much was for the pleasure of the other women. Or was this more amateur porn from Pookie Michaels?

There was so much I didn't know about my sister, and watching her fuck half of Portland was only confusing me more. In her homemade videos, Ash could appear submissive but still somehow seemed, usually, to be in charge of her own degradation. I could never tell for sure if she was asking to be violated—to be spanked by that fancy shredded whip while one woman thrust her fist in and out of her at a rapid-fire pace—and how much was Ash ceding control. If she confused pain with pleasure, which was this?

If the scene didn't involve my sister, I could maybe find it arousing, this lesbian version of *Behind the Green Door* or all-female *Story of O*, but with my dead sister the center of the erotic attention, I found my body and emotions a jumble of contradictory responses.

The ringing phone broke my concentration, and I felt simultaneously relieved and disappointed. Finding Father on the other end immediately shifted my feelings again, ratcheting up the disturbed dial.

"Megan, your mother would like to see you this weekend," he announced, calling Tabitha my *mother*, though she never curried to the title herself. "Please come to the house for dinner tomorrow."

"I can't," I said wondering why he said she was *mine*. Was I somehow responsible for her? If someone had to own her, why wasn't it him? Why didn't he call her his wife? "I'm working this weekend. Sorry."

Expecting him to accept work as a perfectly reasonable excuse and quickly hang up, I was surprised when he hemmed and hawed for a moment before blurting, "Well, listen, young lady, I need to speak with you." Oh no, the young lady bit. It must be serious.

"Okay." I waited for the rebuke.

"I understand you've been seeing this Shane person who was your sister's, um *acquaintance*."

Ah, acquaintance. His language made me pine for the days when the euphemism was *friend* or *roommate*. Acquaintance was even less intimate, suggesting even less of a relationship between the two parties.

"And how do you know that?" I wondered if he stumbled onto a blog while searching for porn. I wanted to scream at him, insist Shane was my *acquaintance* first, but even I knew that wasn't true. Everyone and everything in my life somehow belonged to Ash first.

"It's been all over the news. We've fielded quite a few media calls at the firm. There seems to be a great deal of interest in your, uh, illicit relationship with this Shane character."

Father couldn't bring himself to say "woman" because that would be admitting his daughter, both of his daughters, were big ol' dykes. Still, the way he hissed "Shane character" made me cringe.

"I don't think who I see is your business, Father. I am twenty-four, remember?"

"Listen, kitten, your behavior reflects poorly on me, our family, and my business. And since Shane is an actual suspect in Ash's murder, you could be playing Russian roulette with your life. You need to stop seeing her immediately. Out of respect for your sister, and for me. I won't lose another daughter that way."

He spat out the last line with a vengeance.

What way was that? Did he mean he wouldn't lose another daughter to murder or to lesbianism? At this point I wasn't sure. I tried to suss out his motivation. I couldn't tell if he was convinced that Shane was Ash's killer, despite the lack of any proof or motive, or if he only cared about appearances, and as long as a cloud of suspicion hovered over Shane, he didn't want me to go out with her, not even with an umbrella.

"Father," I stammered.

"No, I said drop it. You'll do as I say and end this now." And with that final pronouncement, he was gone. I laid there, stunned at his misdirected admonitions and the sheer irony of watching a filthy sexcapade on screen starring my dead sister while Father warned me to dump my girlfriend for fear Shane would ruin or corrupt me in some indefinable way. If anyone was corrupting me, it was Ash. She hadn't let something as minor as being dead and buried keep her from exposing me to the dirty truth. Father probably just wanted to prevent another scandal, or maybe he was even trying to protect me in his brusque and paternalistic manner. Was this his way of saying, "Megan, I love you"?

I hardly wanted to give my father the satisfaction of doing what he'd ordered me to do. But then again, if Father wanted to express his concern for me, shouldn't I take advantage of it? I couldn't imagine it happening again anytime soon.

I debated the idea for a few minutes and decided that I would indeed go to the estate this weekend. I wanted to find out if Father knew something I didn't about Shane's guilt. Maybe he had some kind of proof. I mean, I couldn't believe Shane had actually killed Ash, but I'd always felt she wasn't being entirely honest with me about that night. Shane was always angry and cagey when Ash was brought up. Maybe she did have something to hide and I let lust blind me to the fact.

When I arrived at the house, it was Tabitha who looked excited to see me. She was subdued, still beautiful, but definitely unmade, much of her usual artifice stripped away.

"Welcome home! Are you staying for the weekend?" She was speaking in a high voice. I didn't realize I was so badly missed out here at Casa Caulfield. More often than not, the only greeting I got was from Maria.

"Yes, Father insisted I visit so I decided to make a weekend of it. How are you?" I asked politely.

"As good as can be expected I guess," Tabitha said cryptically. "I have something for you." Tabitha ran to the library and came back with a small framed text. As I read I realized it was a weathered copy of George Eliot's poem "Two Lovers" with a scrawl across the bottom.

"Wow, Tabitha, I…"

"You know this was your sister's favorite poem." I didn't know my sister read poetry at all. I thought I was the only literature buff in the family. I assumed Ash was all TV and tabloids, never venturing beyond twentieth-century pop culture. I should have known, reading her journals, how literary she was. I felt sad at the umpteenth reminder that I didn't bother to know my sister at all.

"I had a scout looking for an autographed copy of the poem over a year ago. You know it's really rare, and well, he called me last week and asked if I still wanted it, and I thought that maybe you would enjoy it as much as Ashley would have."

I smiled not just at the gift but at Tabitha's habit of calling my sister by her birth name instead of her nickname. Suddenly, it was endearing more than annoying. The one positive thing I'd discovered after my sister's death was how lovely a person Tabitha was. I could never see her as my mother, but now, in the wake of all this misery, I could see her for the woman she was. This was probably what Ash saw, too.

"I love it, Tabitha. Thank you." It was ironic how, in the wake of my sister's death, I no longer hated her hand-me-downs. Or Tabitha.

After some small talk, I ventured off to my room, adorned as it always was, and pulled out one of Ash's journals for a quick read before the family dinner. Reading about sex in Father's home now felt beyond perverse.

❖

March 21

I try to explain it to Cynthia tonight, the meaning of punishment with kisses, and she doesn't get it, how I first said it to Father after he spanked me so hard my butt blistered and Mother sent me to stay at Grandma's house for a week, but by the time I came back Mom was already dead, the cancer so swift and sudden it took her from us almost overnight.

That night of the spanking, oh how I wished for an alternative, something more loving than the belt. I finally got it. I didn't know then that kisses could be punishment, so it's all the more ironic now that I see they can be. But simple, stupid Cynthia didn't get it either, and I don't have all the time in the world to explain life to her. She's with me constantly, always trying to touch me, to hold me, to own me. I tell her again and again, I don't want her like that. I just want a friend, but she whimpers and whines so much I relent and I spread my legs and let her have a piece of me, the piece I've shared so often and so easily it seems unfair to not let Cynthia have it too. After all, I do so want a friend, someone to confide in. But before I even finish, I stare at her big silly grin and her wide eyes, and I wonder why on earth I let her do that again.

The worst part is when she comes up to kiss me, smelling like musk and pussy and desire and I'm reminded that a moment ago I was making a shopping list while pretending to come just so the poor sod would be happy. If she were my friend, she wouldn't need me that way. She'd help me be happy without diving into my cunt every time she came over. As it is, we do this over and over again, and I always hate her afterward. I get annoyed and I make her leave and she storms off until the next time, when we repeat the cycle all over again. I'm just afraid now that Cynthia will upset all of my plans with The One. I'll do almost anything to get The One back, including leave all of Daddy-O's money behind. Cynthia is probably the only one who knows, so if it all goes awry, I'll have doe-eyed Cynthia to blame. Poor sod.

I'd always known that Cynthia and Ash were close, and I'd obviously caught them having sex together, but now I was seeing just how close the two of them were. I needed to talk with Cynthia. She probably knew Ash better than anyone. Certainly better than me.

Tracking Cynthia down wasn't hard. She still lived in the same house in Portland's Montavilla neighborhood that was listed in Ash's address book, and when I called she was eager to see me. Which, given the circumstances, I could sort of understand. After all, she'd been Ash's best friend and we'd hardly spoken since the funeral. She was probably looking for closure. Maybe she wanted an update on the case. Still, even taking that into account,

Cynthia seemed oddly eager to reconnect. I wondered what kind of ulterior motive she might have up her sleeve.

"Hi, kiddo." Cynthia met me at the door. "Oh, I'm sorry. I mean Megan. What are you now? Twenty-five?"

She didn't give me a chance to answer.

"It doesn't matter. I'm sure kiddo is no longer appropriate. It's just that—old habits die hard. It's good to see you," she said, putting her hands on my shoulders, holding me at arm's length, and looking me up and down. "You look fantastic!"

I wondered if Cynthia was just saying that because she recognized the clothes I was wearing as Ash's.

"Did you do something different with your hair?"

I blushed, happy she noticed, but a little nervous that Cynthia might confuse my getting my hair done by Ash's stylist as an effort to look more like my dead sister. That was hardly the case. I mean, he obviously did great work, and I had every right to pamper myself once in a while.

And my appearance couldn't have changed more in the last eighteen months than Cynthia's had. Far from the feminine artifice I recalled, Cynthia was now clean and fresh faced, not a hint of makeup on her. Either this was her I'm-not-going-to-see-anyone-so-why-dress-up casual wear or Cynthia had butched it up a bit too, wearing Carharts and Chuck Taylor sneakers. From the soil ground into her pants, smeared on her face, and sprinkled in her hair, it was clear Cynthia had just been out rolling around in the dirt. Or possibly toiling in the garden I could see out back.

Never in a million years would I have pegged Cynthia as the kind of woman willing to do her own dirty work and household maintenance. Maybe it was the help's day off. I couldn't have misjudged her that completely, could I?

"Well, you look great, Megan. Please come in. My girlfriend and I were out gardening, so excuse the mess."

After a few requisite pleasantries, I just blurted it out. "I'm trying to figure out what happened to Ash, and since you were her best friend…and lover, I thought you might be able to tell me something I didn't know."

Cynthia looked more perplexed than resolute. "I'm not sure I have anything that could help you. I already told the police everything relevant. I mean, they interviewed me three times."

I heard her words and the inference behind them. Cynthia didn't know Ash had left me her diaries. She probably thought there was so much I didn't know about Ash that she didn't know where to begin. That's why she hedged her responses. "You never know," I said, repeating lines I'd drifted to sleep to. "Even the smallest thing could help." TV detectives and criminologists always seemed to say that, as though random, irrelevant information was the most likely to solve a case. *She washed her hands after going to the bathroom? Oh my God, I know who killed her!*

Cynthia shook her head and shrugged. "Sorry."

Why had she wanted to see me if she was just going to blow me off? She knew Ash better than almost anyone. Did she think there was nothing, not a single bit of information that could be useful? I tried a different tactic. "What did you tell the police?"

"Just that I knew she had dated a bunch of people but no one serious. She was, um, sort of detached with her lovers. But like I told them, I couldn't imagine any one of them going so far as killing her." Cynthia paused.

"Cynthia, you and I have never had a serious conversation, so why don't you start off by telling me about how you and Ash got together?"

"Okay." Cynthia acquiesced, and the story began to spill out of her, first in single words and then in a rush of sentences and paragraphs, recalling their first months as friends in high school, bonding in the backseat over boys, and later, bonding even tighter with the boys out of the picture. Their relationship quickly crossed the boundary between friend and lovers. "She was my first," Cynthia admitted.

"First sex? First love?" I wanted clarification.

Cynthia chuckled at the naiveté of her youth. "Both really."

"You both took boys to prom. It wasn't mutual?"

"That I don't know." Cynthia shook her head and was silent for a moment, musing. "But yeah, we dated boys throughout college, always keeping our own relationship under wraps. It killed me to see her date those guys. I never knew if she was fucking someone else or not, and she always kept me in the dark. Still, I had a pretty good guess. And high school was excruciating because of it. But I didn't dare tell anyone for fear my parents would find out, we'd be separated, and I'd get shipped off to boarding school."

After high school the duo went to the same college, but instead of coming out together, Cynthia stayed closeted, still pining for my sister, while Ash bedded half the cheerleading squad and gained a reputation as a one-woman recruiting dynamo for the gay-straight alliance.

"Ash loved to turn women, and she was good at it too—always beat her quota and took home the best prizes," Cynthia joked, trying to deny her true feelings about Ash's philandering, but you could see them in the frown lines around her eyes. It was the first time I noticed how much older than Ash Cynthia had seemed. Had loving my sister prematurely aged this woman?

"And where were you with all this?" I prodded. Then I wondered why. Why was I making her relive these painful memories? Did I really think they would help find Ash's killer, or did I have some ulterior motive? Did I think Cynthia deserved to be punished? Hadn't she been through enough?

"Waiting mostly," Cynthia said. "And doing whatever Ash wanted me to do."

This apparently involved Cynthia having a lot of sex, just not always with Ash. Cynthia said she loved Ash but that my sister used her as bait for other sexual conquests—with women and men, though Cynthia preferred the former—and rewarded Cynthia with the occasional hump to keep her in line.

"Ash was a very damaged human being," Cynthia whispered conspiratorially. "I realized long ago that she was completely ignorant of the pain she caused other people. It was like she had been hurt so bad that she no longer felt emotional pain and she forgot that other people weren't numb like her. Maybe she did push someone too far one day and she got what she deserved."

I was mortified that anyone would say something like that out loud. Cynthia must have seen my stunned face, because she sat back and corrected herself. "Oh, that sounded horrible. I don't think she deserved to die, I just mean, she sure pissed off a lot of people."

I tried volleying a few more questions at Cynthia but didn't get anywhere and was starting to believe that my sister wasn't too far off the mark when she'd implied Cynthia wasn't very bright. Clearly, she was hiding something, she was a world-class liar, or she was rather dumb. What could she stand to gain by not telling me all that she knew? Or was it that she was afraid of the truth?

I felt like she was holding back, the way Shane did whenever the subject of my sister came up. It was making me angry. "Look, Cynthia, I know more about Ash's secret life than you might think. I've seen the DVDs, I've read the journal, and I know where the bodies are buried, okay? So why don't we drop the charades?"

"You've seen it?" Cynthia looked around nervously. My God, who did she think was watching us now? She leaned in and whispered in my ear, "Her sex diary?"

"Yeah. Like I said, I've read her diaries. I found them when I cleaned her apartment."

"No." Cynthia shook her head insistently. "Not those. She has another one. A secret one that nobody knew about but me. It was small." She illustrated its dimensions with her hands. "Ash carried it with her everywhere. She liked to record gossip, you know, about other people that nobody else knew? I don't think she was blackmailing anyone, or anything like that, she just liked to have information other people didn't. She told me one time it gave her this sense of power, being privy to other people's secrets."

What was the point of Cynthia describing the alleged book when she could just be telling me where it was?

"Where did she keep it?" I asked.

"I don't know." Cynthia shook her head again. I wondered if she would tell me if she had it. "Ash kept it somewhere under lock and key, but not at the apartment. That's all I know," she added, lying again.

If I ever wanted the truth, I'd have to come up with another way to entice it from Cynthia. Or Shane. Were they keeping her secrets, or their own?

I was beginning to feel like I missed so much of my sister's life I was unraveling more than just the mystery of her death. But what was I looking for now? And if I found that journal, would it hold the clue to who killed Ash? Or just open up another Pandora's box?

CHAPTER ELEVEN

June 30

It's not bad enough that kiddo watches me through the blinds, spying on me like a jealous lover, but now I'm quite certain someone is following me at the oddest times and places. I don't know if I'm crazy or if it's true, but I feel like I should hire a private investigator to follow me around and find out if he's the only shadow I have. Maybe an ex is stalking me. Or maybe The One has people following me. I can't tell what's real and what's not real anymore. I go off to the parties and can be there at all hours, but when I leave I always feel another set of headlights behind me. I've hidden my real journal, the one that unlocks everything, so that nobody can find it without me wanting them to. I'll never give it up either. It's the key to my power, my control over the situation.

I think the real problem is, I don't know if I deserve to be safe or not. Surely if I cared about my future, I might take different actions with my life, might do something different with the information I've been given, with the power that I can master. But I don't see a future for myself, not really, not the way I feel now. I have no one

I can trust. Not even Megan, I know, because I see the way she looks at me, like I'm some treacherous tramp she wants to spit on in the street. I'm not the sister she once loved. I'm just a whore, the harlot of Lake Oswego.

So if someone is stalking me, I just hope they don't get in the way of the truth. I know I'll end up in an early grave, but as long as the truth comes out, I'll die a vindicated woman.

I stood in the kitchen with the smoke detector blaring, one of my tits hanging in the sink under a stream of cold water. I was making chicken for dinner and burned my boob on the oven. Hard to believe, I know, but somehow I decided it would be a smart thing to cook oven fried chicken and sweet potato fries in a low-cut shirt on a summer day. The house was steaming, my shirt popped open, and out plopped the boob and, well, there I was at the sink just as Shane raged through the front door, slamming it behind her.

"What's wrong?" I asked as gently as I could. Shane had been under a shit storm at work lately, and every day her mood was worse than the one before.

"I got canned."

"What? Why?" Shane loved that lit journal, and she'd been working sixty hours a week to help keep the thing afloat. Why would they just fire her?

Before she even registered the question, I knew the answer. The publicity around Shane's possible involvement in Ash's murder had been fierce, although no law enforcement agency had gone on record to link her to it. Her firing was just another link in the chain of events that was colluding to shove our relationship onto the wrong track. *We* were fine, but all this external pressure was too much.

Between the media, our jobs, Father, the bloggers, and Cynthia, well, there didn't seem to be a soul alive who thought Shane and I should stay together. I thought this pressure could explain why so many celebrities broke up in the face of constant media scrutiny.

"What are you going to do?" I asked quietly, hoping to coax Shane into talking.

"What do you mean, what am I gonna do? What can I fucking do? I can't take this, I really can't, Megan." Shane broke down crying then, a touching sign of her humanity I so rarely saw these days. Long gone was the girl who played connect the dots on my skin. Shane was a changed woman. Harder, bitter, indifferent.

More like Ash. More like me. I had changed too. I was no longer the sweet, inexperienced girl I was when that summer began. I spent my days hiding who I was and my nights trying to reenact things my sister had done. I'd watched Ash's sex DVDs obsessively, spending dozens of hours in front of the screen, always worried the next scene would co-star my current girlfriend making nice with my sister.

Video quality being what it was, I could rarely tell faces, masked and covered as they were. Occasionally I recognized someone I knew. I swear the players included a classmate, a friend's mother, a teacher, and the girl down the block who never said boo to me. I didn't know what to make of the silent videos, each one with the sound intentionally recorded over with dark concertos. If there were secrets on those videos, I'd never decipher them, not orally at least. Well, aurally, that was.

My mind wandered so much I forgot about my boob, the chicken, Shane's pain. I put it all away and led her to bed, where she cried in my arms until we both fell asleep.

The next morning, I broached a subject that had been nagging at me for weeks. "Ash had another journal. A secret one she hid somewhere."

I hoped it might draw Shane into conversation, but I was not expecting the outburst that followed.

"Oh for fuck sake, Megan, your sister is dead and buried. Can you please fucking let it go?"

"I can't believe you could say that to me! This is my sister we're talking about. I owe it to her to uncover everything I can about who she was and what she was going through, and maybe, if I'm lucky, figure out who killed her."

"That's the police's job, Megan. Let them do it!"

"How can you sit there and say that? When letting the police do its thing is why you're being reviled in the press. If we're ever going to clear our names, we have to figure out who killed Ash!" I was yelling now, trying hard to get through to her.

"I hate to break it to you, honey," Shane drawled. "Ashley was most likely killed by some enraged lover, or someone's jealous husband or girlfriend. Your sister was a tramp and she pissed off a lot of people and clearly one of them killed her. End of story!"

"How dare you!" I shouted at the jab, aghast at what Shane had the nerve to say to me. I was sincerely shocked. This was the woman I'd professed my love to, and here she was suggesting my sister deserved to be brutalized.

"Megan, it's just that you're obsessed with Ash. You're reading her journals, acting out scenes from her films. It's not right."

"Gee, you never complained earlier when I was acting out scenes from her home movies. Was it only good if I'm acting them out for you, then? Or are you worried I'm getting too close to the truth, Shane?"

Now it was her turn to be shocked or act it. Well, fuck her, then. I'd go find that sex diary myself. I'd find my sister's killer myself. I didn't need her or her bullshit any more. I grabbed my purse and my keys and headed toward the door. Shane had other ideas.

She caught my arm and yanked my shoulder back. "Wait!"

"Fuck you," I snarled.

"Hold on, I didn't mean—"

"What? You didn't mean I was obsessed? You didn't mean my sister was a tramp who deserved to die? What didn't you mean, Shane? Or was it you didn't mean I should stop acting out scenes from the sex videos? What is it?" I flailed my fists ineffectively against her broad chest. I wanted to hurt her. I wanted to run down the street shrieking and pulling out my hair. My sister was never coming back. She was dead and no one, especially not the people closest to her, seemed to even care! It was so wrong.

Shane folded her arms around me and pulled me into a bear hug. "I'm sorry about all of it, babe. I didn't mean what I said. I'm just overwhelmed."

And as with all of our arguments, Shane and I went from zero to sixty to bed within minutes, neither of us ever really forgetting or forgiving what had been said. We had angry, reckless sex that left me slightly bruised, but still horny in the morning. But by then I'd forgotten the sheer animosity I felt the evening before, and as I watched Shane sleep, I thought again about how beautiful and serene she looked with the morning light shining on her face.

"You're watching me again," she mumbled without opening her eyes.

"That's true." It was a game we played on the weekends. I woke early, I watched her sleep, she caught me and feigned embarrassment. Today, though, she rolled over and wanted to talk. It made me immediately suspicious.

"Where should we look for this infamous sex journal then?"

"You're going to help me? I thought you didn't believe in me."

Turns out she did believe in me, she just wasn't sure she believed in the existence of this secret journal. We made plans to head out to Lake Oswego after dark so we didn't have to run into the parental units. Father would be agog to know that I was still seeing Shane—after he'd made it so clear that he was ordering me not to. So avoiding him and Tabitha was critical. Tabitha had been lovely to me, calling me at least a couple dozen times since the murder, always to talk about nothing really. I enjoyed those conversations, which felt both meaningful and vacuous at once, always on the precipice of something, but what I never knew. It was usually me who rushed her off the phone as I was on my way to something more important, even if that was often just another page of Ash's diaries. I still wasn't sure she'd keep my secrets from Father, so I'd kept her at arm's length. Even so, I was trying to be more mature, and I'd slipped into calling her Tabitha instead of stepmonster. Our relationship had finally transcended animosity. But old habits died hard.

That night, Shane and I dressed in black like cat burglars and drove out to the estate hoping the lights would be out by the time we arrived. All but Maria's were, and I was fairly confident our sixty-something maid wouldn't get up and run out to the pool if she caught a glimpse of our flashlight.

I snuck over the fence, almost musing to myself about how ironic it was Father never installed better security after the murder. That's how men are, though, they always feel safe. Or maybe he felt like it was too late, the worst had already happened. Still, he often left Tabitha alone in that giant house, when that should have given him pause. Like I said, men were overconfident in everything. He probably thought a security system was a sign of weakness or failure. Or worse, he thought Ash deserved what happened to her. Whichever, tonight it was a godsend because we pulled open the back gate, grabbed the hide-a-key under the rock where Ash always left it, and walked right in.

It made me wonder if the murderer did the same thing.

Shane would have made a terrible jewel thief. The moment we got inside the pool house she started shaking and fidgeting. I don't know what she thought might happen, but I could see from the light of the moon that her face was glistening with perspiration. Between that and the nervous twitch, I felt like I was breaking and entering with that disabled comedian, the guy who can't stop the tremor in his hand.

Shane was one step from hysterical laughter when I whispered in her ear, "It's okay, babe. We'll be out of here in a minute."

"Yeah, I know, but being here creeps me out. I haven't been here since that night."

And then it was me who was totally creeped out. A year and a half after my sister's murder, we were standing on the very site and I was finding out that my girlfriend was here the night Ash was killed. I knew she hadn't been telling me the whole story. So was that her engine that gunned? *What the hell?* I was wondering what I was thinking returning to the scene of the crime, at night, with a woman some people suspected of being Ash's murderer. Was I secure in my convictions about Shane's innocence?

I expected Shane was omitting something, but I had never imagined it would be something as critical as her being here that night. Or had I? That night I was sure I heard her motorcycle. Wasn't that what I'd wanted her to disclose all this time, even if I didn't want to admit it to myself? But what else had she kept from me? What if she had more to do with my sister's death than I was willing to acknowledge? Could she have changed her mind about coming with me because I was getting too close to the truth? Was it her idea to lure me out here in the dark of night and dispose of me too?

"Oh God." I didn't realize I sighed it out loud.

"What?" Shane said urgently. "What's wrong?"

"Oh, nothing. I'm just overwhelmed. Can you go wait for me by the car?"

Shane didn't budge. She stared at me quizzically for a moment then finally relented. "You sure? I can handle it. I'm better now."

"No." I urged her to leave, to return to the car and keep an eye out on the street in case we were followed. I told her it would be safer for us that way. Plus it was true, standing here in the place where Ash died did overwhelm me. So little had changed since that night, save for some bloodied tiles that had been replaced.

As soon as Shane stepped outside, I locked myself into the safety of the cabana. It was disturbing that locking myself into a crime scene felt safer than being outside with my girlfriend. I used my flashlight to meander through the rooms, rummaging behind shelves and under the dresser. Then I went back to the old cedar closet, a storage space that had always been kept padlocked shut even though it held only old prom dresses and Mother's wedding gown. Maybe it now held Tabitha's gown too. I wasn't sure. In the years after our mother died, Ash and I would pick the lock with a bobby pin, climbing in Mom's dress and pretending we were about to be married to the man of our dreams.

I wonder when Ash stopped imagining the man of her dreams and imagined the woman instead. Or had she given up on matrimonial love by the time she switched to girls? She was certainly a cynic by the time Tabitha came around, though the two of them hit it off instantly. In those early years, Ash and Tabitha were thick as thieves, shopping together, sharing clothes, and sunbathing topless when Father and the gardener weren't around. By the time Father was constantly railing on Ash to keep her clothes on, Tabitha had stopped joining her, but still Ash never once ratted the stepmonster out.

That was uncharacteristically selfless of her, I thought. Maybe she was just loyal to the stepmonster. Who knows? Either way, the contents of this closet might or might not contain Tabitha's dashed dreams but they would always primarily belong to Ash and me.

I picked the lock as swiftly as I had at fourteen, cracking open the door and inhaling the cedar that flooded the room. When I was younger I wondered why every closet wasn't made of cedar. In rainy Oregon, I learned, that wouldn't be a wise thing to do.

During those years of trying on Mom's dress and playing "I do," we discovered that the green-brown-gold flecked shag carpet had a section at the back that pulled the entire rug up and exposed a floorboard that wasn't attached to the others. We felt like Indiana Jones opening it the first time and discovering inside it was another opening to the left that was too small for a man's hand but perfect for my tiny girl hands. Inside that was a pile of notes, a beer can, and a half smoked doobie on a feathered roach clip. Clearly, we weren't the first teens to live at Casa Caulfield.

Though the notes were cryptic kid stuff, we envisioned they were love letters hidden by a tortured princess or Anastasia, before she remembered she was the queen of Russia, or whatever she was. We made up all sorts of silly games, creating lavish stories about the kids who came before us and why they hid secret messages in the floorboards here. We smoked the joint but left the Billy beer can intact, in part because Ash said it would taste revolting and part because it was like our homage to those teens before us and their secrets. When Mother died, she left us without any traditions. Father never cared for tradition, or celebrations for that matter, and Tabitha was from a piss poor family she couldn't wait to escape. That's why she married Father, they said, to get out of the house. I wasn't sure if that was true, but it would make sense because she didn't bring a single family tradition with her. She also didn't bring a single family photo to the house either, at least not as far as I'd ever seen.

Even though Mother left us without any traditions, carrying on the secret hiding space from the kids who came before us became the one shared custom we carried on. Over the years we honored it with more pot, birth control pills, love letters, fake IDs, and bad report cards. We even put our diaries there as kids, which made it all the more ironic that I didn't think to search there earlier. It was so long ago, I couldn't imagine Ash having a secret so dark she still had to use that hiding spot when she had the privacy of an adult.

So I cracked open the hole and shoved my hand through the small aperture, the sides scraping my arm and pushing splinters inside my palm. My fingers crawled along, feeling their way past the dirt and dead bugs until my hand stumbled on the thing I had been looking for all along. A leather bound diary and a bottle of perfume. The image on the front of the bottle was faded but clearly that of a woman wearing tall boots and nothing else, and the brand name, Nana de Bary, sounded oddly foreign, but when I spritzed a little in the air, it smelled like my big sister was there in the room with me.

CHAPTER TWELVE

The real sex diary of Ashley Caulfield, September 14

It happened last night. It hasn't happened in years, but it happened last night and it was terrifying. Well, wait, let me fill you in on the back story. Who knows if in my drug addled state I'll ever remember these things in weeks to come. I like Pat. I don't mind doing scenes with Pat, my pudgy, bisexual photographer. He bottoms for me and takes my photos and usually sets up great scenes with me and other women. Pat is always great at finding masochists who want to be bullied and pushed around, yelled at and tormented by a bitch like me. Sometimes I'll play with men, too, but Pat almost always sets me up with chicks probably because with men I might take it one step too far and Pat knows that. I like to shove my playmates around, show everyone who is boss, at least in the dungeon if not in real life. In real life, they're all doctors and lawyers, and I'm, well, what exactly am I? A spoiled rich girl with no ambitions. These women don't care. They let me be an absolute pig about it, too, pushing and berating them until they're about at the end of their collective ropes, always leaving them wanting and begging for me, for more, for sweet release. But that's not my job. I don't

*have to worry about their needs because the scenes Pat
sets up for me are all about me, baby. And last night
was no different.*

*Except it was. You see, last week I let one of Pat's
bitches switch with me. I've been ratcheting things
up for months now, so much so that vanilla sex with
any one person is just a huge disappointment. Well,
except The One. But I can't have that, now can I? The
One isn't really available, isn't always there. I have to
get my rocks off somewhere, so I turn to Pat and the
scenes and the little beggars that I get to push around
with my paddles and pleasures. Then I let one of the
women switch with me. I let her try to top me. I wanted
to acquiesce, to play a good bottom, to let her control
me. But it became so real, and I was flashing back to
those days, that first day, and I couldn't think, couldn't
breathe, couldn't remember my safe words, so I just
started shrieking like a howler monkey, right there in
the middle of the dungeon. Everyone around me freaked
out and ran to me, unlocking my collar and cuffs and
trying to soothe me.*

*I went home mortified at losing control like that,
but then I realized how great it felt afterward. I relived
terror and came out the other side of it lighter, calmer.
So the next night I went back and bottomed, this time
with a pro. I had a dominatrix tie me to the table and
drip hot wax down my back, and I felt sensations up and
down my spine, but mostly in my clit. I was frightened
and aroused, and I pushed that panicky feeling back in
my throat and down to my sex organs, and soon my fear
was blatant and energizing.*

*I had Pat set up a few more encounters this week.
All for play parties where I bottomed, sometimes solo,
sometimes with a group. Mostly, there were women, but
occasionally there was a transguy there too. The vibe*

was the same, everybody too cautious to push me over the edge. And then last night, what always happens, happened again. I got bored.

What does a girl do when bondage and domination are no longer enough? When sweet kisses and loving caresses do nothing? When the only way to get off without The One involves taking it deeper and darker until you can't recognize yourself anymore? Because that's what I'm doing, but who knows how far I can take it, you know?

Pat says he can still conjure up a scenario that will scare me into an orgasm—they don't call it the petite death for no reason, you know—so I'm letting him come up with something that'll really knock my PVC socks off.

I was in the middle of telling Shane about Ash's sex journal, the one that's more shocking than any of the others I'd already read, when a funny look washed over her face. I hoped to God it wasn't turning her on, because I could only take things so far and reenacting my sister's S&M play wasn't exactly the direction I was hoping to go.

"What?" I demanded. "Did you already know this?"

"No, it's not that. It's just…" Shane trailed off as she looked away. "I did play with Ash once."

"What do you mean you played with Ash once? You did S&M with her?"

"No, I, um, she asked me to be a part of a sex game with her and someone else and it was kind of humiliating and I don't want to talk about it. I just wanted you to know in case she wrote about it or something."

"What did you do?" I was not shocked. There was little at this point that truly shocked me.

"I just said I don't want to talk about it." Shane was adamant. "Look, I'm just not going to talk with you about my sex life with your sister."

Wow, so they had a "sex life," did they? I was not sure then if I was relieved to not hear the juicy details of their tête-à-têtes, or if Shane's reluctance to share meant she was harboring a secret far worse. What that might be, I was not sure, but the mere fact that she participated and enjoyed one of Ash's humiliating sex games revealed a great deal about Shane, almost none of it good.

But I was not the sweet girl who fell in love with Shane what seemed like a lifetime ago. I was a chick on a mission, a sexual being in my own right, and I had Ash's journal to keep ciphering. Fuck Shane. I was going to find Pat, this bisexual photographer who played S&M Cupid for my sister, and uncover what he knew about her death.

Tracking down Pat was as easy as finding Cynthia. His studio was set squarely atop the gay district in Portland, amid what local queers call Vaseline Alley. But getting him to sit long enough to talk with me was a different story.

Pat insisted on working while we spoke, so I was following him around all day as we went from one photo shoot to another. It started in his studio with a beautiful woman in a diamond necklace wrapping a striped yellow-and-black snake around her body. It was breathtaking watching her, though the whole scenario begged for a Freudian interpretation. I got the answer when I realized the vixen posing nude in front of us couldn't have been more than fifteen. Society and the youth culture, what a fucked up duo.

After the snake girl, we did a location shoot for a gay couple's wedding photo. It was quick and clean and this time everyone was clearly way over twenty-one. The last shoot of the day was at a nightclub called Holocene where a troupe of chubby drag queens and Rubenesque burlesque performers hosted a benefit party for something called The Fat Experience. Not sure if it was something like Esalen or Scientology, I kept my distance, marveling nonetheless at the surety of the large-bodied folks who were prancing around the stage. To be comfortable in one's skin must be so nice. Refreshing.

Finally, at midnight, Pat turned to me and asked, "Well, chica, waddya want to know about your sis?"

I was flummoxed at this point, so the questions gushed out of me like an overactive waterfall. None of them actually stuck because I was saying them so fast even Pat couldn't understand me.

"I have an idea," Pat said, holding up the shush finger in front of his lips. "Why don't I take you to the club where your sister liked to play?"

I had never been to a play party or a dungeon or a power station—descriptors Pat used on the ride over, but none of which were listed on the sign outside, which read, "Love Inc. A Private Retreat for Couples." It was a basement party palace that was only open to private membership. I quickly learned that in the world of sex, "couples only" meant no solo men. Women were always welcome to come alone, especially if they were the pulchritudinous kind.

I followed Pat down an ordinary wood-paneled hall, past a sign in station where we showed our driver's licenses and he a red members card, and we were on our way to the back where people were mostly just milling about in various states of leather and undress.

"Well, Pat, who's the babe?" one middle-aged woman asked, leaning in to hear the answer. "Oh, I should have seen the resemblance. I'm Natalie." Middle-aged pushed her hand toward me in greeting.

"Nice to meet you." Was this how it was in a sex club, I wondered. Shaking hands with folks who were thirty years older than me, not a speck of sex anywhere in sight? But Pat pulled me away and started showing me around the club, back to the solo and group play rooms, where finally there were couples and groups of average-looking people in different scenarios, sporting leather, uniforms, or nothing but boots, each offering up scenes of submission, domination, and bondage. It would be salacious to Father, but nothing that was remotely shocking to me, especially not after reading Ash's journals and watching her DVDs.

After Pat disappeared into another room, I wandered around more, mostly just watching the action unfold in front of me. A few of the women looked vaguely familiar. One was that tall blonde who had the threesome with my sister. Another could have been the woman from the group encounter with the bird beak masks. But in this setting everyone looked somewhat recognizable yet wholly strange. One woman even looked a bit like my stepmother, though I was certain she wasn't. Tabitha would never be at a place like this. The very idea of it made me titter with giggles.

"Enjoying yourself, I see?" The brunette from another video sidled up to me.

"Oh, I was imagining someone here that wouldn't dare step foot in a joint like this."

She nodded and smiled and I could see she was quite attractive up close, when not visualized through pixilated video, though I was having trouble imagining her without a ginormous dildo strapped to her thigh. I guess this was the downside to seeing so many folks naked; real life could be a bit of a letdown. No wonder Ash had to keep ratcheting up the tension more and more just to get off.

"You'd be surprised at the people who do come in here," the brunette drawled, her short hair flipping up at her collar, a little shaggy bang showing off her eyes. "Is this your first time?"

"Indeed it is. I'm Megan."

"I know. I recognize the resemblance." Like everyone else, she clearly knew my sister. She didn't offer up her own name, nor did her demeanor betray curiosity. "What brought you here? If you don't mind me asking."

"I'm trying to find out who my sister Ash really was. She came here a lot."

"Do you know why she came here?"

I shook my head. I was mildly curious, oddly fascinated by these naked, blithe people and their willingness to act out roles of power and submission. The scene fascinated me the way many parts of Ash's world had come to fascinate me, but I still couldn't say I knew why Ash came here, to this particular place, to this particular club, or why she stopped coming here.

"She was working through something in her past. I can't say any more, but I think she'd be glad to know that you knew that about her." The nameless brunette began to turn, to walk away from me, but I stopped her before she did, pushing myself in front of her as nicely and calmly as possible.

"Wait, what do you mean? Please tell me what you mean. I have to find out what was going on with her before she died or I'll never know who killed her."

"Listen, kiddo, some questions are better left unanswered. Your sister's death may just be one of those questions." That was it. I had had enough.

"Oh, for the love of God," I said, my voice raising just a pinch. "Why does everyone around me speak in fucking riddles these days? I feel like I'm Alice falling down the rabbit hole, and every time I try to get a logical answer out of someone, something cryptic comes out of their fucking mouth. It's like living with Mister Miyagi, for fuck's sake. Don't tell me to go east or west or feel the wind or learn which questions weren't meant to be answered. These cryptic answers might be fine for the Mad Hatter, but they're driving me batty. I have to know what you're talking about. Please just tell me."

She looked stunned, which I hoped was a good thing. She didn't let me know, but steered me rather forcefully down a darkened stairwell that led down another flight below the ground-level club. I began to worry. Where was she taking me? What did I know about this woman, or Pat, for that matter, or any of these people? *Nothing.* Nobody knew I was even here. For all I knew this woman was a serial killer, leading me to the fruit cellar to carve my body up like a Halloween pumpkin.

Before our feet hit the ground floor, she stopped and turned toward me, whispering in my ear, "Do you really want to know?"

"Of course," I said with more certainty than I felt.

"Okay," she said and calmly laid it all out. "Ash was abused as a kid. She was trying to work through it with SM."

No, she wasn't. She couldn't have been. How could she have been abused and not told me?

"You're lying. She lied. I don't believe you." A dozen denials rushed forth all at once.

"I figured as much. She shielded you from it." The woman was calm, collected. Why was she lying to me? Maybe Ash wanted attention so badly she told the women here she was an abuse victim.

"Who supposedly abused her? I would have known!" We shared a room until Mother died, had all the same uncles and priests and deacons as each other. It wasn't possible.

"I don't know. All I know is that she was sexually assaulted as a child and took it upon herself to protect you from the abuse. We don't normally let abuse victims play at our parties because it can be hard for them to distinguish pleasure pain from what was thrust upon them, but Ash had already gone through therapy, had moved beyond her abuse to this different place. This was her safe space to work out her self-injurious behavior without harming herself. We watched over her to make sure she never went too far."

But she did go too far at some point, didn't she? Something must have gone seriously wrong because Ash was dead and I was in the basement of a sex club talking about abuse allegations with a woman with pierced nipples, buttless chaps, and a belly harness.

"I have to go," I gasped before sprinting up the stairs and out into the night air, choking back tears and swallowing oxygen like I'd been underwater or buried alive. I couldn't breathe.

Was Ash *really* sexually abused? Who could have done such a thing to her? All our uncles were old men now, our church elders all the same old men that we had as kids. Nobody sprang to mind. That was the disturbing thing about pedophiles, how easily they blended into society. But why had it never come out over all these years? And who would have dared harm the favorite daughter of Bradford Thomas Caulfield? Surely whoever did such a thing must not have known Father, because if they had they would have known they were risking their very lives by touching Ash. I had absolutely no doubt that if my father had found someone even looking at Ash that way when she was just a child, he would have literally choked the life out of them.

I didn't recall any of our family friends going missing, or any male relatives dying in suspicious circumstances. Wasn't that proof that it didn't happen?

That night I fell into bed without a word to Shane, exhausted from a day of revelations and debauchery. Was this how Ash felt? Sexually stimulated one moment, embarrassed and mortified the next? It left me with both a terrible sense of shame and a burning desire to return as soon as possible.

CHAPTER THIRTEEN

It was the fifth round of a knock-down, drag-out match between Shane and me.

In the weeks since the sex club fiasco I'd been back at least half a dozen times, usually for research but sometimes for more personal reasons. I didn't tell Shane, but she sensed something was up. The girlfriend usually knows. I almost told Tabitha once, too. I ached to tell someone about my sexual odyssey, but the fear Father would find out was too great to make that leap.

Pat had taken me under his wing, introducing me to the other clubs in the city, sending me off alone or with his other friends to the girls-only affairs by the college, instructing me on going incognito to the city's rarified mixed-gender bathhouse, even accompanying me to the couples swing parties where a girl like Ash—or me—could bounce from room to room only accepting pleasure if she were so inclined.

Pat liked to swing, with girls, with boys, and even though Ash mostly liked women, I could see why she put out for Pat, too. He was all about pleasure, pure hedonism. It was thrilling, living only for that moment, not just that orgasm, or the flush on skin when someone touched me, not even for the sheer joy of having a roomful of people lust after you, if only for a night. It was the moment, being surrounded in that moment by nothing but sexuality. It might be vacuous, living among these denizens of the night, planning nothing beyond my next trick. But I found my new world wholly intoxicating. I was no longer Megan Caulfield, bookworm and little sister. Here I was Queen Christina, Helen of Troy, Xaviera Hollander, Erica Jong. I was the happy hooker, the coffee, tea, or me girl, every erotic icon I had ever read about in literature, and I couldn't get enough of it.

There was an emptiness inside me that hadn't been filled, couldn't be filled until all of me was filled, and believe me, in these darkened nameless sex clubs, I was finally getting my fill—in every sense of the word.

Unfortunately, there was little room for Shane in my new life and she seemed fully aware of it. She never once asked to join me in these adventures, and though she used to complain about my dullness in the sack, now she couldn't wait to have me scale things back sexually.

"You're spending too much time in these sex clubs, Megan," she yelled. "You're so far into that world that you're becoming just like your sister. Do you want to end up like her too?"

"My God, Shane, I would think you would care more about me than to threaten me like that." I was livid. How dare she try to suppress my sexual exploration with scare tactics!

"Babe, I'm not threatening you. I'm worried about you. You go out every night, you stay out all hours, I never know what you're doing out there. I feel like you're not just trying to find out what happened to Ash, you're trying to become Ash."

Maybe I was. Maybe I liked the feeling. The truth was, I was enjoying the sexual explorations more than I wanted to admit. But Shane, well fuck, Shane was the one who was bored with our old sex life, so I'd think she'd be happy about these changes, maybe even proud of my sexual expansion.

I was enraged that she wanted to thwart everything now that it was no longer convenient for her. I didn't want to be under her thumb, but she was determined to keep me there. It was like living with Father again, and the whole thing made me scream and cry all at once.

"You know, Shane, this is all rather rich coming from the woman who trolled around my sister like a tabby in heat for weeks on end. If you loathed Ash so much, why did you spend every waking moment hanging on her?"

Shane stared, full of bitterness and rage, but clearly mulling her words carefully. "Megan, your sister was a whore. I hung around for the same reason everyone else hung around. Probably the same reason people hang around you nowadays. Feel better?" With that carefully metered yet bitter retort, Shane just turned and marched off, slamming the bedroom door behind her and then the front door, as she left the house. I heard the engine gun and I knew she and her stupid motorcycle were gone for the night, if not forever, and I threw myself on the bed crying like I had the day we buried my sister. It was a long, tortured night.

I was sitting at Father's office, the gnarled oak desk a rather foreboding presence there. I didn't know why he commanded my company, but I was there, the ever-dutiful daughter, sitting in the room I was usually banished from. In the very few times in my life that he had asked me to come here, I never noticed before how large and imposing the desk was. I was tempted to make an analogy about my father and this beast of office furniture as my mind was doing its best to not focus on why I had been summoned by the man I so rarely had contact with.

So instead, I wondered why the CEO of a lumber corporation didn't even have a computer. Did his secretary do all his typing? What about monitoring the stock market or something? It was baffling. Combined with his charcoal leather executive chair—also about three times larger than the visitor chair I was seated in—the giant desk and dark wood walls made me feel like I was tiny and insignificant and powerless, like a third grader in the principal's office. I supposed this worked for Father, making his visitors and employees feel powerless and malleable, but it made me wonder about his confidence, his virility, even his desire to appear the authority at work and home.

Father was always so powerful, so foreboding, that I never dared cross him. After my mother's death, he detached himself from the family, sending Ash and me to boarding school for a time, and removing every indication of Mom from the home. I didn't even know where all her stuff went—maybe to the Junior League thrift store—but a lot of our childhood memories went with it. The dinosaur drawings, the Popsicle stick pot holder, that stupid clay ashtray, the family photos from the Grand Canyon— all of them were gone when we came back from that winter at Hollingsworth Academy.

We never once spoke about her after she was gone. Father wasn't an emotional guy. No, scrap that. He was a clinical guy, and stern pragmatist, so I figured his aloofness made it so he was insensitive to a fault. He married almost immediately after Mom's death, when Tabitha was nineteen. It was the first time Father did anything that the country club set might frown upon, but I learned early on that at least half of his peers—the male half—were more than just okay with it, they were envious.

My best friend that year told me Father was having a midlife crisis, but he certainly never talked to us about it. Maybe he was. Maybe my mother's death jolted him awake and he decided to bank on the youth and beauty of a woman only two years older than his daughter. But the truth was, he remained an enigma to me, and honestly, to everyone around us. If he had a breakdown and turned to Viagra and teen pussy as the cure-all for watching my mother die, I'd never know it. For us, she died, we were sent away, he got a new wife, we came home. Nobody in our home ever discussed emotions after my mother died, least of all him.

When we did have talks with Father, they felt much like they did today, with me sitting in his office, surrounded by the trappings of masculinity, waiting to find out exactly what he or Tabitha thought I had done wrong this time.

"Your mother isn't happy about the shenanigans." He didn't bother filling in the gaps, knowing that with a little information I'd hang myself.

"I've asked you not to call Tabitha my mother," I retorted. The woman graduated high school the same year I arrived there, for fuck's sake. Why did he have to push this all the time? "And I'm not sure I know what you're talking about."

"I know about your visit to the pool house, Megan. You're certainly welcome to visit our house any time you like, but it's not appropriate for you to be breaking in, in the middle of the night, with some hooligan in tow. I want to know what the hell you think you were doing?" He was trying to sound reserved, but I could sense a darkness underscoring his words. It was my house, too, until last year, and now it was *their* house and if I didn't plan to come to Sunday dinner I was somehow breaking in. Well, in this case I did, but still, it was the principle of the matter.

"Fuck. I did not break in!" I protested a bit too loudly.

"Megan," Father exclaimed in an odd monotone whisper. The yell whisper I liked to call it. "We're in a professional setting here. I don't know what your workplace is like, but that's not appropriate language at my company."

"I'm sorry. It's just frustrating. I didn't break in. I had the key and I let myself in. Is Tabitha upset, or are you upset?" He ignored my questions.

"And what were you doing there? Why did your *friend* need to be there?" Father said friend like it was an insult, a word that should be spat out in certain circumstances. I wondered what he envisioned when he imagined Shane. Did he simply see the woman corrupting his daughter, or something far more sinister? Did every mention of her and me lead him back to sex? Another irony, given that so few things lead us to sex nowadays.

The conversation continued on for what seemed like hours but must have only been a few minutes given Father's tight schedule. I managed to stave him off with a confession that I was missing Ash and wanted to feel close to her again—which wasn't untrue—and I promised not do it again. If I came to the house again I'd have to come alone and plan to stay for dinner per Tabitha's request. By the time I got back to my apartment, all I wanted to do was throw myself in a hot tub, pop in some schmaltzy meditation CD, and wash away the whole episode. Someone had other plans.

I didn't pay heed to the unlocked door. It was not uncommon for either Shane or me to walk out without locking it. It was Portland, after all, not Mexico City. In fact, I was slightly thrilled at the discovery, because it could mean that Shane had been back. But as I raced through the unlocked door, not even thinking about whether I should take her back after the way she spoke to me, my foot snagged something and I fell headfirst onto the glass coffee table. As I lay there, moaning, I glanced around, focusing, realizing that someone had torn the place apart. I couldn't tell if anything was missing, but everything was tattered like a scene from an old detective movie.

Except I wasn't fishing some dead hooker out of a reservoir and following Whitey back to the smoking gun. I was just a chick with a girlfriend who hated me and a dead sister and an apartment that generally looked like Ikea furnished it completely. Today the whole place was…annihilated. Every drawer upturned, clothes, CDs, tchotchkes everywhere. The pillows and sofa cushions had been slashed so violently I couldn't help think about Ash, the knife, her body, that night. Was this a sign of rage, or was I reading into it? Were those cushions supposed to be me?

I didn't even race to the bathroom to vomit. I just knelt there, bewildered and frightened and throwing up on an area rug that once looked like a Lichtenstein painting and now felt like an eerie reminder of how unsafe I was.

Did Shane do this? Why would she come in and do this? When I could finally control my sobbing, I called her, not the police, which I know was the mark of a hysterical woman. I just couldn't believe she could hate me this much. Within twenty minutes Shane was by my side, calling the police and holding me as I rocked back and forth on the carpet, still sitting next to a pool of my own filth. She sounded genuinely concerned when I called, though I didn't recall even stringing together more than a few sentences before sobbing again. My gut instincts were right... well, to a point. Shane had been there that morning and packed her few meager belongings in a duffel she was planning to return. She swore to me that she didn't molest the apartment. That must have been left to a burglar, but why on earth they picked me I had no idea.

As Shane and I made our way through each corner and drawer of the few rooms, we tried cataloguing all that could've been worthwhile to an ordinary thief—DVD player, stereo, laptop, iPod, Gucci bags. Shit, thieves have been known to take Calphalon pans and faux jewelry, but none of that was gone, not even the diamond ring I got for my high school graduation gift or a giant Louis Vuitton suitcase that belonged to Ash. In fact, nothing was missing. Nothing at all, except two of Ash's tattered old diaries that were sitting on my nightstand (next to a pricey Jonathan Adler lamp, even).

The horror of what might really have been going on hit me: Ash's killer knew I was on to her. Or him. The killer knew I was getting close. Hell, I didn't even know I was getting close until this very moment when I realized that my home was burglarized, torn apart piece by piece, all in search of Ash's diaries.

"Oh, my God!" I heard myself shout as I darted to the vanity. Ash's other diaries, including the one I dubbed The Real Sex Diary, were hidden along with her home movies and the camera. Usually they were all stored in a cubby, hidden in the wall behind a two-way mirror in front of the bed. But one day I got worried and I had Shane fashion a new hiding place in the bottom of the vanity. The bottom drawer had a false front so when you pulled it out, you only saw the usual cosmetics, but behind the drawer was another door that opened into an attached cubicle fashioned into the brick and drywall behind the cabinet. It was ingenious.

I thought so when Shane built it, and now as I was pulling the drawer apart and jamming my hand inside the opening, feeling around for all that was left of Ash, I was convinced that Shane was telling the truth.

Even if she had been there, she knew exactly where everything was—including those diaries and DVDs. If she wanted to get rid of them, she could have done so a long time ago. Since they were still there, that exonerated Shane. So if the burglar was after these diaries, they only got two of them because they didn't know where the rest were hidden. So just who, then, didn't know?

The real sex diary of Ashley Caulfield, July 4

Last night I transcended it all. I feel like things are changing for me from the inside out. I'm getting to the point where I can demand that The One give me everything I need. I'll offer it too. I've taken this to the point of no return. There's no turning back for us now. Last night I was at another play party strapped into a PVC jacket that held my arms close to my chest, while women took turns lapping at my cunt, juices running down the sides of their faces like ejaculate from me. It made me delirious and I came like rockets watching them on all fours begging me for more. Sure, pleasure me, bitches. But at the end, something did click, something did change, because they opened up the jacket and released my arms, and for the first time in a long time I felt a bit free myself. I know I'm going to walk away from this life and I'm taking The One with me. I'm resolved. It's going to happen. I won't let anyone stop us.

Though Shane wasn't responsible for the break-in, she was still insistent on the breakup. It hardly mattered to me, though, because all I wanted to do was absorb myself in Ash's diaries—the ones the burglar didn't discover. I was worse than I was that summer I returned home. At least then I would stop to eat or stare at Ash's beautiful friends from the balcony. But now I was a woman possessed. The first few days I called in sick, but soon my boss insisted I take a personal leave, never once asking me to set a date for my return. I couldn't. I was busy spending every waking moment poring through Ash's entries over and over again trying to understand her all-too-cryptic passages. She must have been serious about her privacy to go to these lengths—hiding diaries, making acronyms and pseudonyms for so many people and places. But what was my sister hiding, and from whom? I felt like the passages in her journals were trying to say something, she was trying to speak to me, as clichéd as it sounds, and I just couldn't wrap my damn head around it.

I had to read and reread and then go to the Internet and scour online groups to unlock each reference. Was Double Down a bar? A person? An action? Who were the Sluts and Squares? When I did discover the answers—that Sluts and Squares was a dance night with queer burlesque performers, for instance, or that the Double Down was a lesbian party or that Bruce was a local drag king or that Persephone was a sexy fire dancer at Rose City Vaudeville—it didn't lead me to any *real* keys to unlocking the mysteries of my dead sister. Everything seemed rather ordinary by the time I unlocked it. So why then all the subterfuge? Maybe she was just too high to make sense? Or maybe drugs made her paranoid?

Even more frustrating were the clues that were entirely indecipherable. Was MILF truly the *American Pie* definition—that is, a "Mom I'd Like to Fuck"—or some other obscure Portland underground reference? Masochistic Intersex Lesbian Femme? Married Illiterate Lesbian Friend? Often times I had to skip an entry altogether as I had no clue what it was really about. Who fucking knows? And until a moment ago I was wondering, who fucking knows if *any* of it even had anything to do with why she died.

And then it struck me. One passage that left me shaking my head not with frustration but with sudden awareness.

The real sex diary of Ashley Caulfield, October 31

> *The One isn't a MILF. Or is a MILF? DDO's MILF, but not my MILF. Hard to gauge what anyone feels inside, though. I know that from how much I want to turn myself inside out, cut a scar from throat to cunt and just turn it all inside out so the whole world can know what I'm feeling, the pain of hiding, of wanting, of holding back, of keeping it all in for so long feels today like way too much. But what would He say? What would they all say? The Junior League. Chaste little kiddo with her nose in a book so long she's lost touch with how I hurt, how I bleed, just like her. Or does she remember? Does she already know? She looks like she knows something. Oh, Mother May I tell? Tell her, tell him, tell them all you're the one offering me a punishment with kisses now?*

Suddenly it dawned on me. It was all perfectly clear in my head, every reference illuminating and concise. Tabitha was The One. As perverted and horrible and wrong as it sounded, I was certain that Ash was fucking our stepmother. I had always read DDO as Daddy-O, a vapid salutation Ash used on our father when she was disobeying. *Isn't that right, Daddy-O?* She said it at the gala before she died, and on the night she was banished to the pool house.

Oh God, as violently ill as I felt that night of the break-in, the night of Ash's murder, the night Shane left, that was nothing compared to how I felt right now knowing with almost sureness that my sister and the woman we both called stepmonster for years were having an affair. In Ash's journals it was clearly going on for at least two years, maybe more. When—no, *how* could this have started? How could Tabitha have betrayed Father? And in the end, was she another of Ash's perverted pick-ups or something more real?

Was she another jilted lover who thought Ash got what she deserved, or was she as torn up as I was about her death? Ash wrote so often about The One, as a sort of ominous force, yes, but also as the sole arbiter of her happiness. Clearly she had a power over my sister—did this also mean she was her murderer?

CHAPTER FOURTEEN

It took me months to begin to understand what transpired between my sister and Tabitha. I could see the path I was on so much more clearly now. I'd dipped my foot in the pool of Ash's sexual depravity and instead of recoiling I'd discovered that I might really like to take a swim. Somehow, just learning of my sister's sexual power buoyed me. Maybe by fucking my way through life, I'd learn the secrets that everyone wanted kept from me. Maybe by recreating Ash's sexual adventures, I'd gain some of that power too.

Daddy-O probably thought learning of Ash's depravity would shatter me, but really, it freed me up to become something entirely new. Three years since Ash's death and I had become a new woman. I was…uncontrolled, liberated like Ash was from all the artificial constraints of polite society and all the bullshit artifice that the average American lived with. My nights had become more exciting than I could have imagined when I was with dull ol' Shane. How ironic that I once wanted her so badly I would have given her anything, even my livelihood. I now thought of her as sort of a dullard, a weight I escaped, awakened not just by Ash's murder but by the passing of the guard in my family. Ash's journals weren't windows to her soul; they were portals to my own.

My bosses at the newspaper could see the change in me right

away, too. They took me off that mandatory leave and, best yet, off that stupid slush pile of crappy freelancer pitches. If I had to read one more misguided pitch on the benefits of Botox, I would have lost it. What part of alternative newsweekly did these writers not understand? Now I was actually out in the field, following leads, writing articles, and making deadlines. In the months following the break-in I had become something of a social butterfly. It didn't hurt that I was the only reporter at that paper who had her finger on the pulse of Portland's dirty underbelly. Well, hell, it was not the pulse my fingers were tapping, but each night I did find a great outlet for my creative juices and in the morning I got to type it up and submit it. I spent part of my time writing traditional news articles and the rest undercover as a culture columnist. I was now PDX's Lipstick Lesbian, the anonymous sex columnist who took on—don't forget up and under—Portland's sexual playground and told the tales. I had topped nearly every girl at the paper and even two of the gay boys played bend over boyfriend for me. Hell, the guys in the mailroom looked like they were going to blow when I walked by now, but I had my sights set on bigger things. It was my boss Cassandra who I wanted to really make cream, but she insisted on maintaining her "boundaries." I figured after a few more of my masturbatory columns she would be putty in my hands, but who could wait?

"Hello, Megan," Cassandra said as I walked through the door to her rather tiny office. I was wearing a pencil skirt and a white oxford shirt that was missing a very pivotal button. I knew she was interested when her gaze fell immediately to my breasts. But she was still coy, still worried about propriety and about the power dynamics of being my boss. Still, she practically licked her lips when she asked me, "What's up?"

God, didn't she know I just wanted to fuck her so badly, right there and then on her white Formica desktop with the other reporters scurrying around outside?

"I just ran across a Goth strip club with a lesbian domination night. Want to join me there?" I twirled pieces of hair around my fingers, flicking the end on my tongue like a Long Island Lolita.

Cassandra was clearly aroused, her face flushed with excitement though, as always, she played it cool. "I'm not sure that's the best use of my time. We're on deadline for the hospital administration story."

I moved into the office, closing the door behind me and flicking the lock sideways. Alone, that was how I wanted us. The boss lady looked like a doe trapped in my headlights, but she didn't want to lose her administrative decorum. I couldn't stop dreaming about pulling off those wire-rimmed glasses and pushing my head down between her ample thighs. I had wanted to see her "O" face for weeks now and I was finally bold enough to just take it this time.

"I'm pretty busy, Megan, if we could..." I pulled her chair from her desk, rolling her lap out toward me so I could hitch up my skirt and straddle it. I put my fingers, still damp from touching myself in the restroom, on her lips and blew, "sh-sh-sh" at her. She resisted, briefly, but by then I had pulled open my shirt and thrust my chest at her. She complied, her protestations a distant memory in the face of my breasts. It was hard to find a lesbian who didn't like me with my shirt off.

I arched my back so my whole upper body leaned against her desk, a pile of pens and paperclips and corporate ephemera stabbing at my flesh, and my legs entwined around her waist like a squid pulling its prey underwater. Though I wanted to force myself on her, playing the top dog in this little erotic battle, I figured the way to win her forfeiture was to let her think she was the one in charge. She wouldn't have to admit defeat that way. And if I had learned anything from Ash it was that if you open yourself up for the taking, someone would always want you.

And Cassandra did. She wanted me badly right now, so with the simple arch of my back I let her know she could have me. And she did. My panties were gone in seconds and her hands were groping me up and down my body. Boss lady apparently wanted me quite badly and I was thrilled to oblige. She tried to talk, but I shushed her again, and the whole move must have emboldened her because within minutes her fingers were inside me, balled up into a delicate little fist that was engulfed by my cunt. I bit down hard on the palm of her free hand to keep from screaming and even still I came with an eruption of grunts and groans that I was fairly certain the entire office had heard.

As I lay there, spent and sweaty, I noticed Cassandra—her clothes amok, her hair askew, her office trashed—looked positively aghast. Apparently she didn't often let passion overcome her—at least not in the workplace—and no doubt by now she was deciding just how she'd spin this to the rest of the staff. It's not easy for the big cheese to live down that she had fucked the newspaper's adventure slut.

Personally, I felt great. There was something about boss lady that intrigued me more than the other tricks I'd had lately, and while it wouldn't stop me from checking out the lesbian action at Club 69 tonight, it might at least entertain me a little bit longer.

"How about we finish what we started here?" I didn't wait for Cassandra to reply. "Let's say around seven at my place." I straightened my skirt and walked back into the newsroom, smiling broadly at anyone who looked my way. *Yeah, that's right, I just banged the boss. How do you like me now?*

"I feel like I have a huge hole in the middle of my soul that I've been trying to fill with an endless parade of women." I was trying to shock Dr. Finnigan. She wasn't really my shrink. She was my psychiatrist neighbor. She had lived in my building for years, but it didn't dawn on me until now how useful she could be in helping me understand my sister a little bit more. I took her a cup of tea the same day I took Cassandra and though I didn't plan to fuck Finnigan, I did hope she was as easy to crack.

"I guess, Megan, the question is why you feel like you have a huge hole in your soul."

Finnegan had to be at least sixty, with long gray and white hair, a slight overbite, and half a dozen cats. She listened intently whenever I talked and never seemed to pass judgment on what I was saying. I did so like trying to shock her though. So far I'd recounted every single sex act I'd experienced and titillated her with a list of aberrant behavior I'd tried out with past lovers, from last week's threesome to a costumed gang bang. Some of the stories were mine; many more were actually entries from Ash's journal. I wanted to know my sister, and if I couldn't decipher her life—or death—maybe Dr. Finnegan could.

So far the lady was unflappable. Even still, these thrice-weekly encounters were becoming mandatory pit stops for me. Work, Dr. Finnegan, a night of fucking, and back again. It was more healing than confession, and Finnegan made a better priest than any I'd seen. But tonight, I didn't feel like going to confession. The hole in the soul was Ash's. I had bigger fish to fry.

"I've got to go, Dr. Finnegan. Big date, you know?" As the graying doc looked curiously askance, I swooped up my stuff and bid adieu. "You're not the only one who likes pussy."

I air-kissed my way out the door and back to my apartment. I'd hardly changed a thing since Ash left it to me. The more I came to know my sister through her journals, the more I found myself becoming the woman she was. One night before going out, I rifled through the bottom drawer of the vanity and pulled out that aging bottle of Nana de Bary perfume, emboldened with a woman on the front—naked, except for thigh high boots. Each time I spritzed Ash's old perfume on me, on my neck, wrists, belly button, it was like a pilgrimage to another time and place. I was venturing outside my life and inside Ash's. By the time I made it to the club, I had to admit, I even looked a little like Ash now. As I strode down the long mirrored hallway leading from the box office to the main showroom, I couldn't help but look fondly in the mirror and watch myself walk by. How many times had Ash gone out like this? How many times had she spritzed Nana de Bary and been inspired by that woman wearing the thigh high boots? Plenty, I was sure because Ash's trench—the only other thing I was wearing over the boots—was saturated with the stuff. I wondered what Dr. Finnegan would say about that?

The real sex diary of Ashley Caulfield, November 12

I've wanted her from the moment my eyes first shone on her. Not in the way I was supposed to, but in the deep, aching need only a woman scorned could have. How could The One be here for him and not for me? I remember making my first move. She laughed and fended me off like the schoolgirl that I was. But I knew then as sure as I do today that she wanted me just as badly as I needed her to. I saw it, hell, still see it in every look she gives me. She tried to hold back, to temper herself, to tell me it's not right. But I knew that desire could only be held at bay for so long. Finally, on one of the many occasions when we were left all alone in that big house, I made my move. Nobody can resist supple young flesh, least of all a woman in a bad marriage to a much older man. I was her passport to pleasure. She was my punishment with kisses.

Oh no, Ash was a bad girl at school today. She can't go on the weekend trip with Megan and Daddy-O. But it's not my fault. You remember how hard high school was, right? After all, it was only two years ago. She tried to fight it, but there are just some things I can do that a man can't, and even at seventeen, I was already an expert at them. She joined me by the pool one day when no one was around. I watched her watching me and I knew she was lonely. He had wronged her, too.

She wanted me like everyone else had, but with her I wanted to give in.

She watched me put suntan lotion all over myself, long, smooth strokes meant to remind her how young and supple and flexible I was. And when I was done, I looked her squarely in the eyes and said it.

"You want some?" You should have seen her face pale.

"Excuse me?" She tried to regain composure, but I knew she was mine right then and there. I pulled my arms under my bikini straps, flipping my wrists upside down so they were bound with my straps and my breasts were bared.

"I'm all tied up. Maybe you can help me out?" Any man her age would have jumped on me right then and there, but The One wasn't easy. She bolted from the pool so quickly I was scurrying after her with my hands strapped to my sides, bikini twisted up around my waist.

I found her in her bedroom and we tumbled onto the bed like two lovers with a death sentence hanging over their affair. I devoured every inch of her until, panting, she begged me to stop. I can still imagine her that day. Her flaxen hair matted and stringy from the pool, her bronzed skin the perfect setting for the most beautiful blue eyes I've ever stared into.

It was never as glorious as it was that first day, but for years it was amazing still. She tried to call it off repeatedly, but each time I threatened to tell Father what she had done. I loved her and was willing to do anything to keep her. But still, she left, again and again. She called my bluff and wouldn't see me, wouldn't touch me, wouldn't hold me anymore. It's a cruel fate, to be discarded by the woman you love.

Each time I believed it hardly mattered. Love was dead and I took refuge in the cunts of strangers, each ignominious hookup a reminder that I'm a bitch, hardened to the meaning of love.

Oh, The One, how could you leave me like this? Last week, I told Pat I needed something really shocking to stir me up. Something more than a coke-snorting wife swap—not that those modern day key parties aren't fun, but I need more out of my adventures. And this time Pat delivered.

Pat had me dress up in this little flapper dress with champagne-colored fringe and a hemline that barely covered my crotch. I wore peep toe Christian Louboutin heels with little black bows. Besides the Nana de Bary perfume, I wore nothing else, not even a bra. Pat put on a large leather mask that covered my eyes completely, and had me follow him to the taxi and then up two flights of stairs at our destination. There was a scratchy old jazz record playing, something that recalled a Mississippi bluesman's deal with the devil, and a lot of hushed whispers. Pat led me to a bed or a divan or something and sat me there, closing a door behind himself. I could hear more talk outside the door but couldn't hear what they were saying. I was tempted to lift up the mask, to figure out where the hell I was, but hadn't I been the one to ask for this mystery?

Soon, the door swung open and there were hands grabbing at me, pulling my arms back and my legs apart, and before I could even say anything my mouth was full too. I didn't know how many people were there that day, or even if they were all women or men. I was never sure how safe I was, though I never bothered to protest. Yet with all that danger, with twenty? Thirty? strangers having their way with me, I was still fairly bored, albeit a bit nonplussed. Who were these thirty strangers who so desired to have me bound and gagged? What were their lives like? Was this a thrilling night or an everyday occurrence? What had they done to be here?

I felt a little out of my body that night. Sure, an orgasm is an orgasm, but when it's not with The One, there's a pure hollowness to my sexual conquests. I fuck 'em and leave 'em, but it doesn't even matter to me. I watched a documentary about Annabel Chong once. The porn star had sex with 251 men. She was all post-feminist, women's sexuality is maligned, and there are double standards. All true, all things I agreed with, but when I watched her banging those dudes, I knew this wasn't about feminism or double standards or even her pleasure. Somebody had taken power away from Annabel Chong and she was getting it back, one hairy dude at a time. I just saw a little girl lost in all that carnality. Not the viper whore her fans wanted to see, but a little girl who probably never meant to take things this far. I recognized the same look when Pat showed me the Polaroids of that night—the hordes of women, each wearing a macabre, smiling carnival masque, penetrating me in nearly every possible way.

I've been behind the green door, and without The One, it's an empty, hollow journey.

I was trying to tell Dr. Finnegan about one of Ash's last journal entries before her death, and I could tell the doc was a little disturbed.

"The thing is, Dr. Finnegan, I'm worried about, um, my sister's ex."

Finnegan was silent, looking pained. "You mean the woman she called the one?" I had refrained from telling Finnegan that The One was probably my stepmother Tabitha.

"Well, yeah. I don't know how much of her diaries are real or fantasy. It all sort of blends together. Hell, in my own life I don't know anymore."

"Do you feel like you're losing touch with reality, Megan?" Finnegan was being concerned, I was sure, but it dawned on me that she was a licensed shrink. If, God forbid, she thought I was slipping out of reality she could probably have me locked up.

"Oh no, no, nothing like that." I backpedaled. "It's just that sometimes I feel like someone is watching me. I can't explain it. In her diaries, Ash says that her, um, The One, hires a private investigator to follow her. I don't really think a PI is following me, but the break-in has me on edge I guess, so I'm always watching over my shoulder. Maybe I'm just as paranoid as Ash was."

Finnegan was thoughtful. "Megan, it's hard to know in our grief and loss sometimes where the lines are between fantasy and reality. I can tell you've gone through a lot of changes this year, and I was wondering if there's a healthier way to channel your energy than reading these diaries and acting out your sister's adventures in the name of journalism."

The old lady was a lost cause. She had slipped into shrink speak and I could tell our next scene would include a lecture about healthy sexuality. That was a little more than I could handle right now so I played down her questions and ducked out of her apartment gracefully.

If Tabitha or Father or even Ash's killer had hired someone to spy on me, I had to figure out what they were after before they found it—or before they killed me to keep it hidden. Moreover, I wanted to give them a little show for their money. I would respond to the surveillance the same way Ash did. I started with my little black book, courtesy of sis.

"Bethany, hi, this is Megan Caulfield."

The voice on the other end of the line sounded sleepy. I pictured sweet Bethany Hanks in her pj's and was even more interested in ticking her off my list. "Yes, Ash's little sister. I was wondering if you'd like to have coffee sometime?"

"Sure, yeah, okay."

We made a date for Tuesday and I was free to dial up another of my sister's old pals. Thus would begin my month of fucking my way through all of Ash's old conquests. Whoever wanted me followed would be getting detailed reports of my liaisons. If the killer was one of Ash's lovers, I'd be getting to her soon enough.

CHAPTER FIFTEEN

The private dick that was hired to follow me was worse than a wise guy in an old *Columbo* episode. Old flatfoot was easy to spot and even easier to lose. If he was supposed to curtail my activities in any way, he most certainly failed. I was so bored with the surveillance that I tried for a while to find creative ways to give flatfoot the slip. I climbed out the bathroom window at Saucebox, took the fire escape at Powell's, hid in a Porta-Potty at the Jazz Fest for an hour. After a while I grew bored with my own shenanigans and decided to turn the tables on him. After a week of following the gumshoe hired to follow me, he just seemed to disappear.

Good riddance. I assumed by now that his reports back to the home office—whoever that client was—had given them enough salaciousness to work with. Subject had sex in parking lot of the Egyptian Club. Subject took a shot of ecstasy and danced at the Crystal Ballroom with twelve different women. Subject flashed me her tits in the men's section of Fred Meyer. I had worked my way through Ash's Rolodex. Tina, Julie, Evy, Beatrice, Leisha, Susan, Ariel—I bedded them all and made sure the private dick was around to see it. Or at least hear about it through the walls of my otherwise soundproof apartment.

The thing that happened, though, was that with all this baseless eroticism, I started to wonder about this woman that Ash pined after for years. How could one secret ten-month love affair affect the next several years of her life? It had always seemed like Ash could have anyone she wanted, her pick of the litter, so to speak, so it made me wonder, what was so damn special about Tabitha, the stepmother I barely knew?

All the signs pointed to Tabitha being the one Ash was in love with, and now, thinking back on the things that Ash had said and done, it seemed obvious, like a giant dumbbell hitting me over the head. Of course it was her all along. But how, why, when? Had they been lovers only that year and never again, or had their affair resumed years later? How could this one woman—a high school educated gold digger Father had married for her youth and beauty—have so enthralled a savvy girl like Ash?

I started to realize that the only way to understand Ash was to understand the woman she was in love with. Had her forbidden attraction to our stepmother gotten Ash killed? Did one of her other lovers fly into a jealous rage when they learned Ash would never love them the way she loved Tabitha?

My quest needed to change. I had to give up my erotic explorations in search of something deeper: the story behind this mystery. Just thinking about it was nerve-wracking, as I realized that I didn't know where to start. And if I hired someone, I was almost positive it would get back to Father. Did he even know about his wife's illicit Sapphic indiscretion?

I needed to find out who Tabitha really was. My Junior League charity-driven stepmother? My sister's true love? Or some sick Sapphic version of Mary Kay Letourneau who preyed on my vulnerable sister? I decided not to trust a PI. I was capable of doing the job myself. So I followed Tabitha from the estate to the bank to the florist, where almost all of her stops were pedantic and typical. She volunteered once a week at some charity, though she was rarely there long enough to get her hands dirty, so I assume she was gabbing and dropping off a check. Poor Father— cuckolded by a young wife who just spent his money and screwed his daughter. Still, there was something captivating about Tabitha and her secrets. She had the ability to surprise me sometimes. Last night, she was at the Q Center at a lesbian literary salon, in a red dress and a black wig. The other day, I watched her walk into Union Jacks, a rather notorious strip club in town. Even when she was incognito she was cautious, constantly looking around furtively, ducking in and out of aisles so she was harder to track than one would imagine a suburban housewife would be.

By now, I realized she was no ordinary housewife. Tuesday's journey was most intriguing. She parked her car at Lloyd Center Mall, got on the railway to downtown, then got off two blocks from the river and walked to a giant glass building called The Pinnacle. I followed her inside at a safe distance, but by then had lost her to the crowds around the elevators. I'd never been to this part of the Pearl District and couldn't imagine whom Tabitha could be seeing there. Again today, she did the exact same thing. Only this time I managed to watch which floor her elevator stopped at—fourteen—and so I followed her up on a different elevator. She was in loft 1411, a corner unit at the end of the hallway, loudly playing that Eric Clapton song "Tears in Heaven" over and over again. I waited in the utility room down the hall, peaking out through the door's tiny hatched window every time I heard a new shuffling, mumbling, or electronic noise, but it was over an hour before I saw anything. Tabitha reappeared in the hall, distracted but red faced and empty-handed, and to my surprise, the door shut on her coat and she broke down crying in the hallway, trapped in the door. Instead of opening the door, she tugged at the camel colored trench, eventually tearing a swatch from it. She turned the knob to make sure the door was locked as she looked nervously up and down the hallway. She looked like a trapped woman, and not just because of the coat.

As soon as she'd rescued her now tattered coat from the door she ran to the elevator as if she couldn't wait to get out of there. Funnily enough, I couldn't wait to get in that apartment. I grabbed the pocketknife thingy from my purse, a rather humorous gift from a former lover who, after I ditched her, suggested that since I had balls I should act like a man. Little did either of us know at the time I could use the little contraption to break into an apartment. Fortunately for me, as I was struggling to open the little knife, I leaned on the door and realized the leftover fabric from Tabitha's coat was wedged in between the door and the lock, so while the lock was set, the door wasn't pulled all the way into the frame. I guess since Tabitha only pulled, not pushed, the knob, she had no idea her lock paranoia didn't pay off. I just pushed the door open and walked right in.

As soon as I did, I felt like I had been hit over the head. I fell to the ground and passed out and when I awoke, it was dark inside and I was cold and damp, still lying on the floor. I gave my eyes a few moments to adjust then I crawled to the table in search of a lamp to flick. As soon as the apartment was flooded with light, I remembered why I was instantly struck. It wasn't a bop over the head that did me in. It was the sight of the larger than life shrine to my sister. There were photos of Ash everywhere, along with some of her jewelry and trinkets, and right at the center of it all were Ash's two missing diaries that were stolen from my apartment. I felt like I was in a horror movie, my own *Silence of the Lambs*, with mementos from the murder victim all around me. Had Father and Tabitha lured me away from the apartment with that bullshit lecture so Tabitha could break in and steal these things? Why were there vestiges of my sister everywhere in this loft?

I stayed in the apartment the rest of the day, rifling through the drawers and cabinets. I tossed through the closet, a veritable smorgasbord of outfits and disguises that would fit Tabitha and my sister both. While the front room was an Ash shrine, the bedroom was an erotic play land. The armoire held leather couture of all sorts, whips, floggers, masks, even a face mask with a leather dildo attached where the mouthpiece would normally be. How could that even work? Handcuffs and feathers and oils and tons of silicone toys were strewn about. There were erotic magazines, including dozens of old copies of a black and white lesbian magazine called *On Our Backs*. There were more than a couple of Pookie Michaels films, each emblazoned with my sister in all her glory on the front of the box. My God, my stepmother knew about my sister's porn past. What else did she know? What did Father know? Had he been here? Or was this apartment Tabitha's secret love nest?

I read through the remainder of Ash's journals, the ones that were taken from me and another I had never seen before. She talked about lesbian play parties and orgies and showing a group of women how to have anal sex with some girl named Tristan. Clearly, there was pathos in there, a desire to titillate and shock the reader—which was who? Tabitha? Me? But so much of it was matter-of-fact. I couldn't help but be turned on, and the one way I could stick it to Tabitha for stealing my sister was to masturbate in her bed. I grabbed the red dress from the other night and put it on. It smelled of Nana de Bary perfume and perspiration and desire and maybe a little shame. Or maybe that was just me. I didn't know, but I was aroused by the magazines and the movies and the orgies and I plunged my hand between my legs and just started rubbing like crazy until I felt everything constrict and I began to scream like a banshee.

Only, this time I didn't feel good afterward. I felt...guilty. I was at the foot of a shrine to my sister, in my stepmother's dress, in the house of a killer—maybe—and I was feeling jealous and aroused and focusing on having an orgasm? What kind of monster had *I* become?

I was so aghast at what I had done, what I had become, that I did the only reasonable thing: I demolished the apartment. I took all of my rage out on the furnishings. Nothing would wash away my guilt like showing Tabitha I was on to her, on to them. I slashed the sheets with her scissors, tore up the sofa pillows, and emptied all the dresser drawers. And then I did the most devastating thing: I destroyed the shrine to my sister's memory. I tore down the photos, threw all the trinkets in the fireplace, and shoved the journals into my bag. I stood there in the middle of the room, knee deep in destruction, and wanted more. I wished I could see Tabitha's face when she walked in and found what I had done.

But like any artificial high, my demolition-fueled delirium ended abruptly and sent me spiraling into the seven rings of self-deprecation. How could I have done what I did? Where did that violence, that *hatred* come from?

I thanked all things holy that Tabitha had not been there during my annihilation frenzy, because I feared what I might have done if she'd been in the room. Would Tabitha have ended up in little pieces on the floor, mixed in with the shredded remnants of her loft? Was this the same impetus that had led to my sister's death?

I did not see Tabitha's face when she discovered what I had done to her loft. We did see each other at dinner not too long after and she was as stone-faced and cordial as ever. Father was as cold and withdrawn. He lectured me about the deficient career choices I had made and the dire economic impact I could expect to harvest from such poor selections. Apparently, Father did not approve of his surviving daughter becoming a journalist, especially not one who regularly wrote about having sex. I had had no idea he even read my column. While he was intent on belittling me, I was feeling rather pleased with myself for having garnered his attention. Who knew that was all it took. Maybe Ash started filming pornos for the same reason. Could she have felt as invisible in this house as I had?

No. I didn't think so. As Father continued to belabor the point, I pushed my chair closer to Tabitha's. In doing so, the back of my hand brushed her thigh. A charge of electricity snapped between us like static cling and then was gone. Perhaps I'd imagined it. Tabitha sat prim and proper with perfect posture in her chair as though nothing had happened. Maybe it hadn't. Or were her cheeks just a little rosier than they'd been a moment before?

"Just how safe are all these…um…" Father struggled for the appropriate couth wording. "These *dealings*? How safe are they, Megan?"

Having long lost interest in his paternalism, I allowed Father to drone on. I wasn't about to ease his consternation regarding my column, but the truth of the matter was that my own interest in the subject was waning. I didn't think I'd be Portland's adventure slut much longer. My passion was too big to be bridled by this city's handful of underground erotic adventures. I needed to be a pioneer in a different way, to open up a new sexual frontier. Just how, I didn't know yet. I imagined Tabitha opening up to me like a desert flower, and it was my turn to blush.

"You don't want to end up like your sister," Father concluded.

With that, I came back to the conversation. "You mean dead on the pool house floor? I can't imagine how that would happen to me, Daddy-O. Don't you agree, Tabitha?"

I winked at her. I was bolder now, too. I wasn't just little Megan, peering out a window at my sister's Sapphic fun. I was the master of my domain and I was the one calling the shots in life now. Tabitha should fear me, because I was on to her little game. Maybe she even wondered why I hadn't already told the cops about her secret double life. But I was keeping something for myself.

Still, when the color drained from her face, I instantly regretted the flippant way I'd recalled that traumatic night. I didn't see Father raise his hand. Rather than warning me, the light breeze on my face only confused me. For a millisecond. Until his palm reached my cheek. The slap was so fierce it rattled my fillings loose and knocked my molars akimbo, the way earthquakes displace fence lines. I was sure it left an angry, crimson handprint behind, far outshadowing the pink of my blush.

Tabitha inhaled so sharply it sounded like the door of

an airplane being ripped off mid-flight and passengers were being sucked out by the vacuum it created. "Bradford Thomas Caulfield!" She shrieked like an angry mother condemning and errant child. "Apologize!" Tabitha yelled.

"I'm sorry," I responded automatically.

Tabitha ignored my authentic act of contrition.

"Bradford." She demanded.

Oh, my God, I realized, looking at the determined set of her jaw, this woman was fucking *hot*. There was something about courageous women that turned me on. No, not courage. It wasn't bravery that lead a diminutive female of the species to stand up to my father and demand an apology—it was recklessness, a sheer and utter disregard for one's personal safety. And I'd never seen anything sexier.

Father did not apologize. He had never once acknowledged personal wrongdoing in all the time I'd known him. When things went so unbelievably wrong that he could no longer ignore them, he always managed to find a convenient patsy to blame it on. I wasn't even that alarmed by the whole scene. I had changed from the kid who wanted only to please her father and fall under the radar, in my sister's shadow. I was older and bolder and less interested in making Father—or anyone else for that matter— happy. I left the table with Tabitha still glaring at Father. They would probably fight for hours over the disagreement, but for me it was water off a duck's back. I needed to get my beauty sleep. I had more spying to do in the morning.

Cassandra, who I bored of after a week or two of tumbling and floor exercises, was just embarrassed enough about dipping her pen in the company ink, that she allowed me the freedom to make my own hours at the paper—as long as they were opposite to her own.

So I started working from my home or the coffeehouse nearly

as frequently as I made it to the office. That gave me more time to watch Tabitha. The funny thing was, the more I followed her, the more intrigued I was by the woman. She was such an enigma to me. Every day there was something unexpected in her life. Last week, it was Taboo—an adult store where she spent an hour, while I waited for her to leave, keeping tabs on the door from the parking lot across the street. What could a woman do for an hour in an XXX video store? Did she actually watch the films there?

Yesterday, she disappeared into a house on 82nd Avenue that had a giant sign outside announcing it as a business named Honeysuckles, and billing itself as a "lingerie experience for men." What the hell was Tabitha doing at all these places? I thought *my* sexuality was aberrant, but hers, well, it made me look like a castoff from *Little House on the Prairie*.

The more I saw Tabitha in these playlands, the more intrigued I became. I wanted to know Tabitha—not just biblically, but as a person. I wanted to know what brought her to these places, what her fantasies were, and who she wanted to share them with. Just who was this woman? Did my sister find out about her secrets? Was that why she was killed?

CHAPTER SIXTEEN

It's an old adage that often the truth isn't what we are truly seeking. I was starting to think that might be the case for me. I had been following Tabitha for weeks now and I was noticing that I was feeling as enraptured by her as other women were over my sister. I started inconspicuously following her to stores, cafés, and even to a strip club, although I could never go in to these venues for fear of being caught spying on her. Instead I hunched down behind the wheel of my rental car, eating Doritos and watching. Watching to see how long she was inside and when she did come out whether she was still alone. Tabitha remained alone—going in and coming out.

Soon, watching from afar just wasn't enough. It was no longer giving me the thrill I'd had when I originally started stalking her. I decided to escalate. I managed to "bump" into her at a few establishments she fraternized, the ones where I could randomly imagine turning up.

To my surprise, Tabitha didn't seem frightened to see me. Quite the opposite. She seemed genuinely happy to have happened upon me. Usually she'd invite me to lunch or out to the house or just to finish up her shopping with her, the latter of which I did enough times that I was starting to enjoy it.

"Try these!" Tabitha smiled and threw another set of trousers at me.

"Ooo, me likey…" I trailed off. Could this be considered spying? When she had insisted upon tagging along with me and I was enjoying myself this much?

After a few shopping trips turned into lunch, I started thinking of Tabitha not as my stepmonster or even a relative, but more like my friend. Okay, maybe not that close, but maybe the intimacy one would have with a sister's ex-girlfriend.

Tabitha was charming and sophisticated, but she could also be really goofy and sweet. When she would pull her hair off her neck, sweeping the long blond strands to the side and titling her head just so to the right, I would think about kissing that beautiful smooth neck. The more I got to know Tabitha, the more I couldn't hate her, and the more I couldn't imagine her as my sister's killer.

Still, in these afternoon get-togethers, which had become an almost daily thing, Tabitha never explained nor did I ask about her curious romps in Portland's sexual underworld. Strip clubs? Porn stores? How could this lovely, soft-spoken woman even venture into places like that, places I was so comfortable with because of my experiences, when she had been saddled with Bradford and the 'burbs since she was nineteen?

Had Ash taken her to these places? Was she revisiting their past? Or were there just…hidden depths?

"Megan, would you like to meet me for brunch tomorrow?" Tabitha was hoping to expand our get-togethers to a weekend apparently. "Bradford's out of town." She instinctively answered my unspoken question.

"Sure, but if Father's out of town, would you like to do something tonight instead? You could stay in the city with me and we can do brunch at Old Wives Tales tomorrow." I wasn't sure why, but suddenly it was crucial that Tabitha stay the night at my apartment. The thought of an all night gab session was more than appealing. I could truly get to know this lovely woman I had never given the time of day before.

Tabitha paused so long I had to ask if she was still on the line.

"Yes, of course, I'm still here. I'd love to get together tonight. I'll be there around seven. How's that?"

"Perfect."

The rest of the day I primped like a prom queen, first plucking, tweaking, and shaving like I had a big date, and later scouring the apartment for anything that would be off-putting to Tabitha. I wasn't wholly sure why I was so concerned with making this evening perfect, but a little part of me was honest enough to admit that during the last week I had thought at least a dozen times about kissing Tabitha. That's it, not fucking her, not capturing her, just kissing her and holding her. I didn't know what to do about those feelings. Did I dare risk this new friendship and my months of investigation just to be honest about feelings I probably would never act on?

❖

Tabitha was ravishing in a winter white mock turtleneck and white wrap skirt. She managed to always look chic enough to have been plucked from the set of a 1940s Hollywood movie. Even better, she came bearing food. I loved that in a woman.

"I hope you still like Thai food. I brought enough to feed us for a week." It was a casual comment, but something about it foretold how Tabitha felt about me too. We were a "we" at least in the recesses of her mind. How did this all happen? "I mean, it's enough for us tonight and to feed you all week."

Her backpedaling did nothing to dissuade me, and I did something I had thought about all week and never in my life imagined I would do. I pulled her close and kissed her, first tentatively, to make sure she didn't scream and run to Father, and then more assertively because it had been months in the making. I didn't care who she was married to. I wanted this woman badly.

I started pulling her clothes off, the wrap skirt the first casualty of my lust. Each other piece, a shirt, a bra, French cut panties—of course—all taking me only seconds to shed. I never stopped kissing her for more than a second, and when everything except her perfect gray pumps had been tossed aside like rubbish, I launched us onto the sofa, still never moving my mouth from hers. She protested only once. She was mine.

I stopped thinking about Father or Ash or Shane or Cassandra or the Honeysuckle Lounge. All I could think about was her perfect creamy skin, the pink just inside her lips, the perfect apricot pucker of hers. I started licking and kissing and nibbling every neglected inch of her: the neck, the spot under her breasts, the crook of her elbow, behind her knees, between her pink little toes. By the time my mouth was back up to her thighs, ready to part what was no doubt a perfectly pink little pussy, she was writhing so much I could hardly hold her down. With her back arched, her belly in the air, Tabitha looked like she was doing a yoga pose. Only I was her yogi and the moaning was more than meditative.

I buried my face in her cunt, lapping and licking and even fingering her with the ferocity of a woman unhinged. As much as I wanted her, she needed me. I could tell at that moment that she had been waiting a long time to be fulfilled again. And I wanted to fill her up. She tasted as sweet as she looked and here, in my apartment, naked and oblivious of the world, we were just two women who needed each other.

Her toes curled a little when she came. I know because her feet were up near my face at that point. Flexible girl. I guess that's what it means to fuck a former cheerleader. Just as I finished she tugged my hair a bit pulling my mouth up toward hers. She had stroked my face while I was going down on her, a simple gesture that spoke words for the level of intimacy we were sharing. This wasn't just a fuck. She wouldn't be someone I could kick out when I was done.

The scariest part was that I didn't think I would want to. But what would that mean for all of us?

CHAPTER SEVENTEEN

The next morning I awoke before Tabitha and sat next to the window wondering what to make of this sudden change in our relationship. We fucked long and hard last night and talked very little, but as I was falling asleep I felt Tabitha gently stroking my face and staring at me. I wasn't sure exactly where to go from there, but the realization that I had fucked my stepmother was dawning on me.

"Morning." Tabitha's whisper roused me from my musings. "Are you okay?"

"Yeah," I lied. "I'm good."

"We should talk." Her challenge hung there, unanswered for a moment.

"Was this a one time thing?" I sounded needy, but I honestly needed to know. Was I another experiment or simply a convenient replacement for Ash?

"God, I hope not." Tabitha laughed, a good throaty, flirty chortle that loosened me up again.

I crawled back in bed with her, gathering her up in my arms and inhaling the scent of her hair.

"I have to tell you something," she said quietly after we lay there for a long time just holding each other. "I was still a teenager when I married your father. I knew there was something there, but I didn't know I was gay. I didn't know really until Ashley told me, and then all the pieces fell into place."

"Did you love him?" It was an honest query.

"I'm not sure. He flattered me. Nobody had wanted me so badly before, and he courted me like Prince Charming. And I thought he was sort of grieving your mother's death and had two girls to raise. So I felt compassion and flattered. He's rich and powerful and he wanted me."

"So you decided to marry him, even though you weren't sure?"

"I rebuffed his advances for quite some time. But, yeah, when someone is flying you to Europe and sending you dozens and dozens of roses and throwing money and jewelry your way, it's hard not to start to look at them differently. I didn't really know who Bradford was until after we were married."

"Do you think he loved you?"

"No. He was cruel in bed, always mocking me for being naïve or unimaginative or frigid. And the verbal threats started early. Once Ash opened my eyes, all I could see was how horrible Bradford was to me. By then, I couldn't stand to have him touch me. Maybe that made me frigid with him. I don't know."

I knew that Father didn't want Tabitha to attend school or have a job, and she was embarrassed about being in that situation in this day and age.

"I was worried about not having the skills to get a job when he did get tired of me," Tabitha continued flatly.

"But if you divorced him, you'd get half his assets, right?"

"No, we had a pre-nup, Oregon isn't a community property state, and Bradford always told me that he could hide his assets because he'd rather see me in my grave before I got a penny of his money."

I didn't know if he could get away with that, but I did know Father had some very expensive, high-powered attorneys on retainer. Sometimes you didn't need to be right, you just had to convince your opponent that it would cost them too much to prove you're wrong. I think that was something Father used to say.

"And then there was Ash and you. All of our friends are your father's friends, so I didn't have anyone to confide in. And my parents just wanted me to make things work out. My parents don't believe in divorce."

Just when I thought I was starting to understand everything, Tabitha announced, "There's something I want to show you." She ran off, disappearing into the front room, and returned with a small crimson tote bag. It made me think of Santa's magic red bag, and when I reached in I imagined it was full of all the things I'd ever asked for but didn't get. When I pulled out some lined sheets of paper, I could immediately tell that the scribbled notes were in Ash's handwriting, and all I wanted to do was drop it back in the bag.

I didn't want to read or even think about Ash right now. Instead of being tied up in knots the way it had been for over a year, my belly was feeling all warm and calm and satiated. But I felt compelled to look. When it came to Ash, I'd never been able to turn away. Sometimes it seemed almost like we were conjoined twins, Ash and I. Maybe we were actually born in a body that was literally connected. Maybe we shared some organs. A heart, a kidney. Then they separated us and because I was so much smaller, they pretended we weren't twins but just regular siblings, born years apart. But I'd never gotten over the separation, being torn away from part of myself, and now I was trying to fill that emptiness, that void where Ash had been.

I knew that wasn't what really happened. But I couldn't always make sense of reality. Sometimes the truth was stranger than fiction. Sometimes what was real was too hard to believe and you needed distance, the kind of perspective you could only get in fictionalized versions of the truth. Like *Boys Don't Cry*.

Not realizing my epiphany might be a lazy God's attempt at

foreshadowing, I examined the papers I'd pulled from the ruby bag. These torn pages, I could see, were the ones missing from Ash's final diary. They really were something I'd asked for.

I started to read, but for some reason I couldn't seem to focus on what it said. I could read the vowels and consonants and form words, and it was in a language and vocabulary I understood, but somehow, when these particular words were strung together to form sentences they stopped making sense.

Sex Diary of Ashley Caulfield, August 27

There's a growing tension around me. I'm not safe now and I know it. I can feel the danger in everything I do, I told my therapist and Tabitha and a couple of girls at my play group about what Daddy-O did to me, that first night, so long ago, when he came into my room, drunk on his own power and reeking of that dreadful fucking Armani. No wonder the stuff still makes me sick when I smell it. I could never fuck someone who wore that now. I'll spread my legs for almost anyone these days but not for anyone who thinks Armani smells good. How long did you want me, DDO? Was it from that first time you saw me in a frilly skirt, running around with my top off, knee-hi socks and pigtails still? Was I a way for you to fuck away your demons, to put the screws, so to speak, to Mother one last time? I look like her, don't I? That night you first took her, as a teenager. Maybe that's what you saw in me? Maybe I'll thank you some day for showing me how cruel people can be, how much a girl can be used if she's not always watching.

You called me Daddy's Little Girl. "Right here, baby, yeah, right here," you said, pushing my hand where a little girl's hand should never have to go. When you rolled off me, you took with me everything I had— my innocence, my trust, my soul. You fucking bastard.

Some day, Daddy's Little Girl is going to make you pay. For all those times you sent me away, because I didn't want to do that anymore, all the times you chased away my friends for all the same reasons. Some day I'll make you pay.

I'm taking your wife with me, too. You don't control my cunt anymore. And you don't own hers.

You'll pay in a way that cuts you to the bone.

Some day. Maybe today, or tomorrow, when your lovely wife slips my ring on her finger and runs off with me. The only cock she'll be taking from now on is mine.

How do you like that, Daddy-O?

There was more to the entries, more than I could handle at the moment. It was proof of what had happened. I realized that my sister's murder *was* indeed a crime of passion. But the murderer has always been someone with a real motive. Tabitha didn't kill my sister. She *loved* my sister.

I must have looked as shocked as I felt because Tabitha pulled me close and began to explain. "Bradford found out. The first time, in the beginning, Ashley told him that she seduced me. I don't know why but he believed her, and God help me, I didn't tell him the truth…that I wanted her so badly I could hardly breathe when she was near me. I just, I just didn't know when I married him that any of this would happen." Tabitha paused long enough that I thought maybe she was done talking.

"You don't have to…" I began.

"Megan, I do have to. I have to finally just tell you everything so you know what you're getting yourself into.

"The first time, Bradford sent Ashley to the Monroe Academy and then he thought it was over. And it was, mostly, for years. Well, it never was. We'd be together once and Ashley would plead and I would cry and she would threaten and I would deny her. But I tried hard not to love her and not to cross that line with her again and again, and after a while she wouldn't put up the fight anymore."

I couldn't help but imagine my sister so powerless in the face of love. She was always so jaded, so hard edged, I was such a selfish kid when she was alive, I never even saw through all that to her pain. "But in her diaries, she says you're going to be together."

Tabitha looked pained. "We were. She came to me when she turned twenty-six, when she could finally access the rest of her trust fund. She proposed."

"Wait." I sat in shock. "Wait." I kept repeating it because I needed this all to slow down. I couldn't imagine my sister, ring in hand, down on one knee, offering her hand in marriage. Was she serious? "She proposed?"

Tabitha nodded. "She gave me a ring, asked me to run away with her, to divorce Bradford and move far away from here. And I told her we would. She just needed to keep up the charade until the end of the summer."

"But you didn't."

"No, I didn't realize Bradford had been monitoring my e-mail and my calls, but he clearly was, somehow he knew we were back together. He had Ashley followed by the same PI he hired to follow you and to ransack your apartment. He always had you girls monitored—I just didn't realize the scope of it until that moment that he found out about us. He confronted us that weekend you were away with Shane. It was that Friday night and he was supposed to be in town for the board meeting. Maria was gone so we were in her room making love and Bradford just threw the door open and started yelling."

The image of Father catching Tabitha and Ash together *in flagrante* would be funny under any other circumstance. I nodded for her to continue. Tabitha was clearly relieved to be able to tell her story.

"He called us deviants and whores, and even though I was pleading with him to understand I did care about him, I just didn't know I was gay when we got married, he wouldn't listen. He just kept yelling over me."

Father was notorious for talking over people. I once tried to win an argument as a little girl, before I realized what a powerful orator he was, and left the room in tears. I tried explaining my chagrin to Ash that night, but all she did was nod in agreement.

"Why didn't you just leave that night, that moment?" It seemed so irrational that they'd stay.

"Bradford said he'd kill us. He was completely enraged. I was terrified. I never thought he'd go through with it. I thought that me calling it off with her would be enough to calm him down. But it wasn't. And I didn't realize until after her murder that it wasn't that he was jealous because I had fallen in love with his daughter."

Oh my God, I realized it as soon as Tabitha said it out loud. Father killed Ash. But not because he had molested her. Because he didn't want anyone else to have her. His warped sense of love meant that Ash was all his, even all these years later.

"He was jealous of me for being able to love Ash in this way." The sick irony of it was that I had this all pegged wrong in my mind.

Ash never planned to tell anyone about Father's abuse. She was savvy enough to realize that, nearly two decades after the fact, and with no physical evidence, it would come down to a "he said/she said" situation, and who would believe a crazy, slutty, society girl raving about some "punishment with kisses" game? Especially when the person she was accusing of these awful things was none other than the highly respected Bradford Caulfield?

"Megan? Are you okay?" Tabitha woke me from my horrible reverie.

"Sorry, it's a lot to take in." I didn't reach out to touch her. I was stunned. "He molested her." I said it like a statement but it was a question.

Tabitha looked down. "Yes. I didn't know until years after I married him. She told me that she let it go on so long, so that you were protected from him. She didn't feel guilt about it. She felt like she saved you from it."

"She saved me…" I trailed off and teared up again. Thinking something and having it confirmed, especially something so heartbreaking as sexual violence, were different demons. Ash had replicated her punishment with dozens of strangers in an effort to exorcise those demons, but that didn't threaten Father until she found true love in the arms of another woman, *his* woman. Tabitha was my sister's one shining beacon of light, and loving her was the ultimate act of betrayal to Father. He would never let the two women in his life usurp him like that. No doubt in Father's mind he owned Tabitha and Ash and even me.

"Do you regret not running off with Ash while you had the chance?"

"Yes. Since she died, I've played out every what-if scenario possible, over and over. I've thought about taking my own life just to get away from all this."

So where did I fit into this whole equation?

"He never would have let her go, Megan. He would have chased us to the ends of the earth. Your father sealed Ash's fate decades ago when he stole her innocence. Since then, she's always belonged to him."

"And me?" I looked her straight in the eyes. "Am I just a cheap replacement for my sister?"

She grabbed me, pulled me close. "God no! Megan, if anything good came out of Ashley's death, it was us, this, that I got a chance to fall in love with you."

"You're in love with me?"

"Yes."

I was silent, studying her eyes, then kissing her lips, then moving down her shoulders to her décolletage. I kissed her breasts one at a time, gently and slowly. She threw her head back and moaned softly, parting her legs as she did, and I made love to her right then and there. Sweet, soft, earnest love. It was surprising how easy it came to us in the face of such horrible tragedy. I didn't need to say the words. I could make her feel, under her skin, down to her bones, how much I loved her, too.

❖

Tabitha wanted me to know everything. She didn't want me to think that she was keeping any secrets about her time with Ash or about Ash's murder.

"We were leaving that night, the night Ashley was killed," Tabitha continued, steeling herself to relive it. "We had packed up a bunch of stuff into a rental car that we had stored in Portland. Nobody knew about it. We were going to take the car and just drive north, since Vancouver was only a few hours away. I'd be out of Bradford's reach, and after my divorce we could get married. We didn't even apply for visas or anything for fear that Bradford would find out. But we figured, once there, it would all work out."

"How were you going to get to the rental car, then? I don't understand."

"Ashley had a motorcycle, actually." Ah, so I wasn't crazy. I hadn't imagined it. "Ashley thought maybe Bradford would chase us down or have the police chase us down. She wanted us to have a motorcycle to get away on. It was maneuverable. We had it down the drive, but when I went out to get it and bring it up, I saw that someone was in the pool house with Ashley so I killed the engine and hid the bike behind the O'Malleys' broken back gate."

Ash must have told her about the O'Malleys' gate. It had been broken the entire time we lived at the estate. The O'Malleys never went back there, and as teens Ash and I would hide behind it to smoke joints with our friends when we didn't want to get caught.

"That was Father you saw?" I knew the answer. I just needed to hear her say it.

"Yes. I heard a scream and I sprinted to the pool, but Ashley was already dead, on the floor at his feet, and Bradford had a knife in his hand. He wiped the knife on his jacket and dropped it on the floor."

Tabitha cried as she recounted falling to her knees and cradling Ash's lifeless body while Father casually stripped off his bloody jacket and shirt, stuffed them in a black garbage bag from under the sink, and slid on a men's shirt from Ash's closet.

"I didn't even think about what he was doing at the time. I was so intent on trying to save Ashley. I couldn't." She was sobbing now.

Tabitha hadn't meant to screw up the forensics of the murder scene. She was honestly in shock that the love of her life had been so brutally killed and that Father was able to be so calm and detached.

"It sounds so awful. I can't imagine." I wanted to offer her some condolence, but what could I say?

"It was so surreal, it was like I wasn't really there in the room, but outside it somehow, watching myself as though I were part of a movie. If it were a film though, Bradford would never have acted the way he did, barely bothering to cover his tracks at all."

Apparently Father was confident in his ability to smooth talk and distract the police or explain away any forensic evidence that remained. There was probably blood on Father's pants, but that was easily explained after he knelt in the growing pool seeping from his daughter's body.

"He told me he did it, after that night, as if I didn't see him holding the knife. He told me time and again that he'd do the same thing to me if I dared leave. Those first few weeks, I felt like I was in a nightmare. I kept thinking that the police would find DNA evidence or fiber transfer or something and link Bradford to the murder. But they never did. Whatever they did find was explained away, just like he said it would be. And the more he got away with it, the more Bradford flaunted it in front of me. He bragged about getting away with murder and told me this was proof he could do it again if I didn't watch myself."

So she stayed. But if she was so afraid of Father, and of his private investigators, I asked, why did she go to the sex shops so frequently? Why would she go to a private gentleman's club to begin with?

"It's not what you think. I've been working there under the table. Since Ash was killed I've been trying to put together enough money to get away from him. They don't ask any questions at the club. I can come in a couple hours while Bradford thinks I'm shopping and make a couple hundred bucks while I wear a wig and a sexy mask. I've got it all in a safe deposit box so he can't trace it. And I know what the PI looks like so I'm always careful to not be seen without disguise."

Turns out even before our interaction, Tabitha was planning a getaway. But how could she let Ash's murder go unpunished?

"I hope he does get punishment, some how. I hope some day he's rotting in hell. But he's Bradford Caulfield. He's a local golden boy—powerful, wealthy, connected. Even with the best of evidence, we both know that men like Bradford rarely get punished."

True. But that wasn't enough for me.

"There's always karma," Tabitha offered.

I had something a little different in mind. In the back of my mind, though, I couldn't stop thinking about one thing: Ash was dead and I was in love with the woman Father was willing to kill over once before. What was to stop him this time? How long before he came after me?

❖

The next few days while Father was out of town were a whirlwind of activity as Tabitha and I hashed through our plans. We each had one last thing to do. I visited Father at his office.

"Megan, you should call first," he chided me before I cut him off.

"Save it. This is the last time you'll see me. I know what you did." Inside, I was quaking, though surely his office was the safest place for this confrontation. Father prided himself on being a captain of industry. There was no way he'd lose his cool in front of his staff.

"I'm sure I don't know what you're talking about." He very clearly knew what I was talking about because his jaw suddenly looked wired shut and his eyes were darkened and his fists clenched.

"I know what you did to Ash. In life and in *ending* her life."

"Well, little girl, if you know what's good for you, you'll stop this gibberish." Father's defense mechanism was to pull out the paternalism. He wouldn't acquiesce easily. I cut him off abruptly. If I didn't play my hand now I might chicken out.

"Here's the rub, Daddy-O." I pulled myself up as tall as I could, pushing out my chest in hopes that it would give me confidence like one of those animals on Discovery who are puffed up with pride. It didn't work. I felt emboldened, but also frightened and small.

"In this envelope you'll find copies of Ash's diary, her secret diary in which she talks about you for pages on end. It's been authenticated already, so don't deny she wrote it. There is also Tabitha's signed affidavit as a witness to Ash's homicide and a release form giving Ash's psychiatrist permission to reveal her therapy sessions to the police investigator still in charge of her case. I'm sure she told him a great deal about her relationship with both of you."

Father started grumbling, a sort of passive protest. It was

unlike him to not be fully cocked in a fight, but perhaps he had been beaten down by this. After all, he killed the one person I think he truly loved, as sick as it was.

"Megan, you don't understand. I loved Ashley—"

"Save it." I interrupted. I didn't care to hear any more of his sickening rationale for fucking and then killing his daughter. "All of these items are on file with my attorney. Should anything happen to either Tabitha or me, they will be sent to the media. Because while you may be able to charm the DA and his cronies, I'm pretty sure the tabloids won't be so kind. And knowing you, losing face will be almost as bad as losing control of your wife."

Father was silent, unmoving.

"Here's what you get in this bargain: we won't go to the police or file suit if you let Tabitha leave now, unencumbered. And as we speak, Tabitha is cashing out the Fidelity International account. We'll be taking that as a sort of one-time-only, good faith alimony payment for her years of dutiful service."

Father's eyes darted to the telephone and back at me. Was he wondering if he could stop the market transfer? Not likely, as Tabitha and I actually cashed it out this morning before he'd have a chance to discover the move. Father had plenty of money. Taking one of his pockets of cash wasn't going to hurt him a bit.

The more important thing here was keeping his attention while Gualterio and Maria helped Tabitha load all her stuff into a tiny U-Haul trailer. It turned out that during many years of faithful service, Maria and Gualterio both witnessed a lot of wrongdoings by my father, and they weren't so much loyal to Father as they were frightened by a possible report to and deportation by the INS. Given the opportunity to help me rescue Tabitha and put the screws to Father, they were both willing to oblige—as long as Father never knew of their involvement. So while I was distracting Father, the real move was happening at home. Or what used to be home.

Since Father was still unmoving, I decided to go in for the

close. "I'm offering you a Faustian bargain here, Bradford." Father flinched when I called him by his name. It meant a world of disrespect to him, I was sure. Good.

"Leave us alone and we'll keep our mouths shut. Come near us, or send one of your goons after us, and we'll make sure the whole world knows what kind of monster you really are."

Father stood, this time making me recoil. I tried to steel myself.

"So, little girl, you think I'm just going to let you run off with my wife? That's pretty rich coming from a spoiled slut who's never even held a real job. What makes you think I'm going to let you two dykes walk off into the sunset?"

"You will if you don't want to be branded a child rapist in the media, and dredge up your possible involvement in a murder for all your high society friends to see. How will business look then? Perhaps I should just go mention all this to your employees outside this door. Think they'll look at you differently? Think that'll affect your bottom line, Daddy-O?"

"You're as much of a whore as your sister was. You got that from your mother. She was a whore, too."

Something inside me snapped and I launched myself off the chair and pummeled him with my fists. He looked as shocked as I was at the violence inside me. I was ready to rail on, buoyed as I was on the truth, but much to my surprise, Father relented.

"Fine, you crazy bitch. You're both whores and you deserve each other. You'd better hope nothing happens to your trust fund." He was back in threatening mode now.

"Well, if you'll recall, my trust fund came from grandmother, not you, and according to my attorney, there's absolutely no way you can ever touch it." Touché.

Father turned, walking back to his phone like it was an anchor in the storm.

"Be gone tonight. I never want to see either of you again." With that, he got on the phone, buzzed security, and told the person on the other end to revoke my key card before I left the building.

Tabitha and I were free. I almost didn't believe it so I drove cautiously back to the apartment, looking in my rearview mirror every few seconds. Was it possible Father would let us go without a fight?

EPILOGUE

It's our four-year anniversary today. I couldn't be more excited. I never thought I'd be in a relationship again, and yet this feels as real and true as anything in my entire life. My whole past, the girls, the orgies, the one-night stands, was all just a dress rehearsal for this. I thought I had tested my boundaries before, but sex toys and multiple partners have nothing on sexual exploration in a committed, loving relationship. I planned my outfit for tonight carefully. A red dress, boots cut up to here, and of course Nana de Bary. It was my sister's favorite and my favorite, but most importantly, it was Tabitha's favorite. When she grabbed me and pulled me close to her, inhaling the scent of my hair and my neck like a monk with the temple incense, I knew she was mine.

I went back last month to the site of where it all happened. Back to the estate, to my room, to the city I ran from. We could go back now. Father would no longer be looking for us, and there was no reason to be hiding out in this little coastal hamlet in Mexico. Father was dead. Heart attack, they said, but I knew, he was heartbroken. He lost all the women in his life years ago. What was left for him?

The estate went to me, so Tabitha and I kept it. Some day, maybe we'll go back. But no time soon. Maria can keep the place occupied. I'm not ready to deal with Father's ghosts as well.

Tabitha and I are too happy to head back now. Tabitha is all I've ever dreamed of in a lover. She is all I'll ever need. I stopped writing about sex parties and downtown dungeons. With Tabitha, every night was a sex party minus the crowds. Unlike Ash, I wasn't the other woman, and now that it's been four years, I'm certain that I am the only woman Tabitha loved.

The estate in Oregon felt so far away from where we are. So does my sister's murder, even the Megan I was when I first came home from college that dreadful summer is but a faded memory, a speck in the corner of my eye that I can never pinpoint but never wash away either. I never once thought, while growing up, that I'd be doing siestas in Mexico, penning a novel in my spare time. Daytime brought mango shakes and surfing and helping Tabby—my new nickname for her—find organic vegetables in the plaza. Some days we just sit on the beach all day, reading sonnets and listening to the waves undulate over the sand. I want to lap up this life with her, to not miss a single minute. I spend my nights under the waning moon over this Mexican Riviera penning my novel, a true story of what happened to my sister. It never distracts me from bed though. Even the compulsion to write, to tell the world what happened to me that summer, is weaker than my desire to make love to this woman night after night. Tabitha is in my arms every night as I sleep, a feeling that I love, a feeling that tells me so much about who my sister was. This was the feeling she was willing to risk her life for. As was I.

They say lesbians experience bed death after a few months, but not us. Even as I was thinking starry-eyed about our years together, Tabitha was on top of me before I could even speak. She was devouring me, hungry from our afternoon apart. Sex and romance and desire all packaged into one holy alliance. I needed her with a ferocious desperation.

She didn't have to push or pull. I was open and waiting the minute she asked. I pressed her head down, moving my pelvis up and down in rhythm to the song on the stereo, each bass drum resonating with my clit. She was hungry and wanted me and I couldn't get enough, so I ran my hands over my nipples, urging her to put a damp hand up here herself. She didn't. She flipped me over and entered me from behind with a ribbed strap-on dildo I'd never felt before. Ah, my gift. I could feel her maneuvering so the dildo hit my G-spot and it rubbed her too, and we both orgasmed simultaneously, Tabitha falling on top of me like a spent bag of potatoes. She was the most amazing lover I'd ever had.

I lay there panting for a moment, salty dampness tickling my tongue. Then I pushed up on her and rolled over, my breasts touching hers in perfect symmetry.

"It's time for a punishment with kisses," I said, wanting her to kiss every part of me for as long as I could stand. And she did, slowly, starting with my lips and lingering in my mouth for what felt like an eternity.

Tabitha moved one hand down under my buttocks and another on my crotch and rubbed in unison in a way that was both relaxing and arousing at the same time. My head lolled back and I barely heard her at first.

What dirty little thing was she whispering in my ear? I listened harder as I came again and again, and I realized what she was saying and it filled me with perverse desire.

"I love you."

"I love you, too," I said before pushing her head back between my legs. I was ready for round two.

About the Author

Diane Anderson-Minshall is the co-author of the Blind Eye mystery series: *Blind Faith*, *Blind Leap*, and *Blind Curves*. She's also the editor-in-chief of *Curve*, the world's best-selling lesbian magazine, and was the co-founder and former executive editor of *Girlfriends* magazine and the co-founder and former editor/publisher of *Alice* magazine.

The multiple award-winning journalist's work has appeared in dozens of magazines, newspapers, and Web sites including the *New York Times*, *Passport*, *Film Threat*, *Utne Reader*, *Wine X*, *Teenage*, *Bitch*, *Seventeen*, *Femme Fatale*, *Diva*, *The Advocate*, *Bust*, *Natural Health*, *Venus*, and E! Online.

Anderson-Minshall is the former president of the board of directors for *Bitch* magazine; a previous Pride Grand Marshal in Oregon, Idaho, and Montana; and in 2006 was named one of PowerUp's Ten Powerful Women in Showbiz, for her work with lesbian filmmakers.

Her essays have also appeared in several anthologies including *Reading The L Word: Outing Contemporary Television*; *Bitchfest: Ten Years of Cultural Criticism from the Pages of Bitch Magazine*; *Body Outlaws*; *Closer to Home: Bisexuality and Feminism*; *Young Wives Tales: New Adventures in Love and Partnership*; *50 Ways to Support Gay & Lesbian Equality*; *On Our Backs Best Lesbian Erotica*; and *Tough Girls*. Anderson-Minshall is the co-editor of the anthology *Becoming: Young Ideas on Gender, Race and Sexuality*.

She and her co-pilot of twenty years divide their time between San Francisco, Idaho, and Portland, Oregon, where they are active foster parents.

Books Available From Bold Strokes Books

Late in the Season by Felice Picano. Set on Fire Island, this is the story of an unlikely pair of friends—a gay composer in his late thirties and an eighteen-year-old schoolgirl. (978-1-60282-082-1)

Punishment with Kisses by Diane Anderson-Minshall. Will Megan find the answers she seeks about her sister Ashley's murder or will her growing relationship with one of Ash's exes blind her to the real truth? (978-1-60282-081-4)

September Canvas by Gun Brooke. When Deanna Moore meets TV personality Faythe she is reluctantly attracted to her, but will Faythe side with the people spreading rumors about Deanna? (978-1-60282-080-7)

No Leavin' Love by Larkin Rose. Beautiful, successful Mercedes Miller thinks she can resume her affair with ranch foreman Sydney Campbell, but the rules have changed. (978-1-60282-079-1)

Between the Lines by Bobbi Marolt. When romance writer Gail Prescott meets actress Tannen Albright, she develops feelings that she usually only experiences through her characters. (978-1-60282-078-4)

Blue Skies by Ali Vali. Commander Berkley Levine leads an elite group of pilots on missions ordered by her ex-lover Captain Aidan Sullivan and everything is on the line—including love. (978-1-60282-077-7)

The Lure by Felice Picano. When Noel Cummings is recruited by the police to go undercover to find a killer, his life will never be the same. (978-1-60282-076-0)

Death of a Dying Man by J.M. Redmann. Mickey Knight, Private Eye and partner of Dr. Cordelia James, doesn't need a drop-dead gorgeous assistant—not until nature steps in. (978-1-60282-075-3)

Justice for All by Radclyffe. Dell Mitchell goes undercover to expose a human traffic ring and ends up in the middle of an even deadlier conspiracy. (978-1-60282-074-6)

Sanctuary by I. Beacham. Cate Canton faces one major obstacle to her goal of crushing her business rival, Dita Newton—her uncontrollable attraction to Dita. (978-1-60282-055-5)

The Sublime and Spirited Voyage of Original Sin by Colette Moody. Pirate Gayle Malvern finds the presence of an abducted seamstress, Celia Pierce, a welcome distraction until the captive comes to mean more to her than is wise. (978-1-60282-054-8)

Suspect Passions by VK Powell. Can two women, a city attorney and a beat cop, put aside their differences long enough to see that they're perfect for each other? (978-1-60282-053-1)

Just Business by Julie Cannon. Two women who come together—each for her own selfish needs—discover that love can never be as simple as a business transaction. (978-1-60282-052-4)

Sistine Heresy by Justine Saracen. Adrianna Borgia, survivor of the Borgia court, presents Michelangelo with the greatest temptations of his life while struggling with soul-threatening desires for the painter Raphaela. (978-1-60282-051-7)

Radical Encounters by Radclyffe. An out-of-bounds, outside-the-lines collection of provocative, superheated erotica by award-winning romance and erotica author Radclyffe. (978-1-60282-050-0)

Thief of Always by Kim Baldwin & Xenia Alexiou. Stealing a diamond to save the world should be easy for Elite Operative Mishael Taylor, but she didn't figure on love getting in the way. (978-1-60282-049-4)

X by JD Glass. When X-hacker Charlie Riven is framed for a crime she didn't commit, she accepts help from an unlikely source—sexy Treasury Agent Elaine Harper. (978-1-60282-048-7)

The Middle of Somewhere by Clifford Henderson. Eadie T. Pratt sets out on a road trip in search of a new life and ends up in the middle of somewhere she never expected. (978-1-60282-047-0)

Paybacks by Gabrielle Goldsby. Cameron Howard wants to avoid her old nemesis Mackenzie Brandt but their high school reunion brings up more than just memories. (978-1-60282-046-3)

Uncross My Heart by Andrews & Austin. When a radio talk show diva sets out to interview a female priest, the two women end up at odds and neither heaven nor earth is safe from their feelings. (978-1-60282-045-6)

Fireside by Cate Culpepper. Mac, a therapist, and Abby, a nurse, fall in love against the backdrop of friendship, healing, and defending one's own within the Fireside shelter. (978-1-60282-044-9)

A Pirate's Heart by Catherine Friend. When rare book librarian Emma Boyd searches for a long-lost treasure map, she learns the hard way that pirates still exist in today's world—some modern pirates steal maps, others steal hearts. (978-1-60282-040-1)

Trails Merge by Rachel Spangler. Parker Riley escapes the high-powered world of politics to Campbell Carson's ski resort—and their mutual attraction produces anything but smooth running. (978-1-60282-039-5)

Dreams of Bali by C.J. Harte. Madison Barnes worships work, power, and success, and she's never allowed anyone to interfere—that is, until she runs into Karlie Henderson Stockard. Aeros EBook (978-1-60282-070-8)

The Limits of Justice by John Morgan Wilson. Benjamin Justice and reporter Alexandra Templeton search for a killer in a mysterious compound in the remote California desert. (978-1-60282-060-9)

Designed for Love by Erin Dutton. Jillian Sealy and Wil Johnson don't much like each other, but they do have to work together—and what they desire most is not what either of them had planned. (978-1-60282-038-8)

Calling the Dead by Ali Vali. Six months after Hurricane Katrina, NOLA Detective Sept Savoie is a cop who thinks making a relationship work is harder than catching a serial killer—but her current case may prove her wrong. (978-1-60282-037-1)

Shots Fired by MJ Williamz. Kyla and Echo seem to have the perfect relationship and the perfect life until someone shoots at Kyla—and Echo is the most likely suspect. (978-1-60282-035-7)

truelesbianlove.com by Carsen Taite. Mackenzie Lewis and Dr. Jordan Wagner have very different ideas about love, but they discover that truelesbianlove is closer than a click away. Aeros EBook (978-1-60282-069-2)

Justice at Risk by John Morgan Wilson. Benjamin Justice's blind date leads to a rare opportunity for legitimate work, but a reckless risk changes his life forever. (978-1-60282-059-3)

Run to Me by Lisa Girolami. Burned by the four-letter word called love, the only thing Beth Standish wants to do is run for—or maybe from—her life. (978-1-60282-034-0)

Split the Aces by Jove Belle. In the neon glare of Sin City, two women ride a wave of passion that threatens to consume them in a world of fast money and fast times. (978-1-60282-033-3)

Uncharted Passage by Julie Cannon. Two women on a vacation that turns deadly face down one of nature's most ruthless killers—and find themselves falling in love. (978-1-60282-032-6)

Night Call by Radclyffe. All medevac helicopter pilot Jett McNally wants to do is fly and forget about the horror and heartbreak she left behind in the Middle East, but anesthesiologist Tristan Holmes has other plans. (978-1-60282-031-9)

Lake Effect Snow by C.P. Rowlands. News correspondent Annie T. Booker and FBI Agent Sarah Moore struggle to stay one step ahead of disaster as Annie's life becomes the war zone she once reported on. Eclipse EBook (978-1-60282-068-5)

I Dare You by Larkin Rose. Stripper by night, corporate raider by day, Kelsey's only looking for sex and power, until she meets a woman who stirs her heart and her body. (978-1-60282-030-2)

Truth Behind the Mask by Lesley Davis. Erith Baylor is drawn to Sentinel Pagan Osborne's quiet strength, but the secrets between them strain duty and family ties. (978-1-60282-029-6)

Cooper's Deale by KI Thompson. Two would-be lovers and a decidedly inopportune murder spell trouble for Addy Cooper, no matter which way the cards fall. (978-1-60282-028-9)